Romancing the Billionaire

CAN'T BUY A BILLIONAIRE
BOOK THIRTEEN

ROSE M COOPER

OSHUN
PUBLICATIONS
oshunpublications.com

ROMANCING
THE
the *Billionaire*

ROSE M. COOPER

OSHUN
PUBLICATIONS
oshunpublications.com

Romancing the Billionaire © Copyright 2022 by Rose M. Cooper
Published by Oshun Publications
9 Old Kings Road STE. 123-1038
Palm Coast, FL 32137
www.oshunpublications.com

Disclaimer

Book design by oliviaprodesign
www.fiverr.com/oliviaprodesign
ISBN 978-1-956319-71-2 (Paperback)
ISBN 978-1-956319-72-9 (Hardback)
ISBN 978-1-956319-70-5 (eBook)

GET YOUR GENRE FIX TODAY! JOIN MY NEWSLETTER FOR MY RECOMMENDATIONS AND UPDATES!

ROSEMAECOOPER.COM

THERE ARE ALSO AUDIOBOOKS!

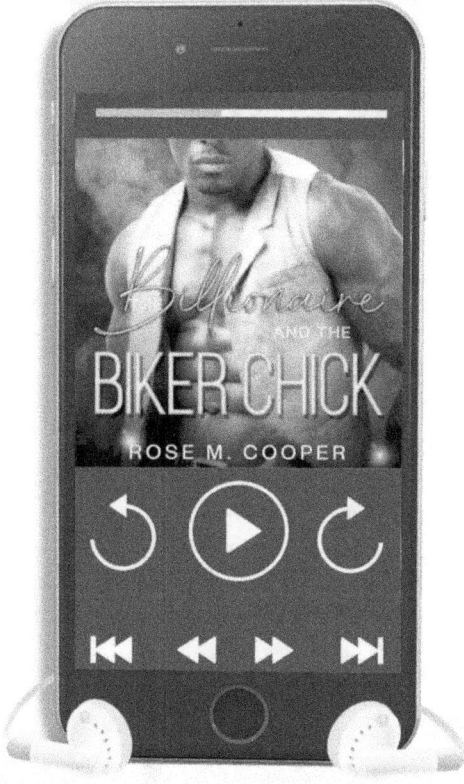

LYRA LOVED the feeling of waking up in her sunny, Mediterranean-style bedroom in the home she had purchased all by herself. After what had seemed like an eternity of university, exams, and internships, she was finally a totally independent woman. Yes, she was mortgaged to her maximum. Still, she finally made it after working tirelessly during her seven-year adult cardiology residency and earning a meager five-figure salary. All her years of hard work, diligent studies, and lack of sleep had earned her the title Dr. Lyra Brunet, and she was ready to enjoy the spoils of her labor.

Everything felt better in her home on Westholme Avenue, in the heart of the Westwood neighborhood of Los Angeles. Built in the 1950s, her house had been designed by a famous local architect and lovingly updated and renovated by the family who had previously resided there. This was a good thing because Lyra was anything but handy. Since she wasn't currently in a romantic relationship, there was no one around to fix the little things that would usually go wrong in her house.

With four bedrooms upstairs, Lyra knew that her home

was an atypical choice for a single career woman. But Lyra loved the trees in her yard, and the whole area felt idyllic. This was the kind of home she had always dreamt of growing up in. Still, her single mother's modest circumstances had never allowed it. Whenever she rode her bicycle through nice neighborhoods as a child, she would look at homes similar to this one and imagined that the families who lived in them were absolutely and perfectly happy. It's precisely what she had pictured for her future happily ever after, and now she needed to find her prince.

She and her mom had always been a team. Her mother was a registered nurse. Now that Lyra worked side by side with RNs daily, she had gained a whole new appreciation for what her mother had gone through, working and parenting full-time with no support. Shift work was tiring, but her mother had made everything seem easy, probably because she loved being a mom. Hopefully, when the time was right, she would experience motherhood and enjoy a similarly strong bond with her daughter.

Lyra felt a twinge in her heart whenever she thought of her mother. Sadly, she had been diagnosed with lung cancer when Lyra was in her final year of residency, even though she had never smoked a day in her life. Yes, she was able to see Lyra graduate from medical school. Still, she passed away before seeing her daughter reach other milestones: buying a home, getting married, and having children. If there was anything that Lyra wished for, it would have been more time with her mother. She had to believe that her mother was watching her from Heaven, forever her guardian angel.

Speaking of angels, she prayed for one to land on her shoulder during tonight's gala fundraiser. When people first met Lyra, they automatically assumed she was bold, confident, and outspoken. She was puzzled by other people's perceptions of her because although she was no shrinking violet, she tended toward the introverted side. Maybe her perfect former ballerina posture made her seem more sure of herself. Although she was a mere 5 feet 4 inches tall, she wore high-heeled shoes for any activity other than a gym visit, which may have made her seem more imposing.

She had an average build, good muscle tone, and youthful-looking mocha-colored skin. Her wide-set eyes were the prettiest shade of brown. Her high cheekbones were in perfect proportion to her wide, inviting smile and rectangular chin. Her nose was broad enough to complement her bright, white smile and also add an air of softness to her face. Lyra had also been blessed with shiny, healthy, manageable black hair that cascaded over her shoulders most invitingly. She was classically pretty in the most unassuming way.

Usually, she wouldn't allow herself the luxury of sleeping in on a Saturday morning since half her weekends were spent on call at the Ronald Reagan UCLA Medical Center in Los Angeles. Lyra had explicitly chosen to buy a home in West-wood because it offered a short commute to her place of work —less than a ten-minute drive in traffic. The office where she saw her patients was located within the hospital itself. Over the years, Lyra had grown very comfortable there. She typically spent four days a week attending to patients in her clinic, teaching medical students one day a week, and working on-call shifts at the hospital.

However, Lyra had asked to take this whole weekend off since the organization she volunteered for hosted their gala fundraising dinner, dance, and silent auction tonight at the Beverly Wilshire Hotel. For the past few years, Lyra has sat on the Smart Heart Start Society board. This organization created nutrition and fitness programs for high school students in the Los Angeles public school system. Society enabled teenagers across a broad economic spectrum to learn about the proper building blocks of nutrition and its interplay with physical fitness. Lyra believed that better educating young people would encourage them to make wiser lifestyle choices after graduation, avoid the typical college weight gain, and lead them into better cardiological health in the long term.

As the only cardiologist on the board, they had asked her to say a few words at tonight's gala, which she absolutely dreaded. She had no problem giving academic lectures, but she felt nervous about tonight's gala for some reason. She stretched her limbs across the crisp white cotton sheets that made up her king-sized bed, allowing herself to luxuriate and enjoy the moment. Her street was quiet, and she heard the muted sounds of chirping birds nested in the mature trees outside her windows. After a few tranquil minutes, she finally willed herself to get out of bed.

She made her way down the wide, winding staircase and padded into her sunny, Spanish-tiled kitchen, where she could hear her automatic coffee maker percolating. The rich aroma was beginning to wake her up and put her in the right mood to start the day. She made a light breakfast of toast, almond butter, half a banana, and a cup of coffee. She felt out of her element, taking an entire weekend away from the hospital. She figured she could probably benefit from a meditative run to relax her and put her in the proper mindset to speak with ease at tonight's gala. When she was done eating breakfast, she filled her water bottle, then went back upstairs to change into a pair of running shorts and a tank top. She laced up her sneakers and took advantage of today's leisurely pace to find her inner alignment. Once outside her front door, she inhaled deeply, and her lungs filled with the freshness of the morning's cool air...and off she went.

Lyra returned home from her run energized and ready to enjoy the rest of her day. After enjoying a long, hot shower, she put on her cream silk robe, wrapped her long, damp hair in a towel turban, and called her best friend Michaela so that they could organize their evening. Since Lyra wasn't currently in a committed relationship—or any relationship, for that matter —rather than attend the fundraising dinner by herself, she bought a ticket for her friend so they could enjoy a glamorous night out together.

"Hello, my dearest darling," Michaela breathed into the phone when she answered. "How much fun are we going to have tonight? How many eligible men are we going to find?"

Lyra laughed. That was the thing about Michaela: she had been boy-crazy during their college days, and she was still boy-crazy at age thirty. It was a mystery to Lyra why her friend was still single when she unabashedly made it her mission to meet men. Michaela Moses was petite like Lyra, with fair skin, a dappling of light freckles across her nose and cheekbones, sparkling emerald green eyes, and full, wavy strawberry blonde hair. She had a perky disposition to match her perfectly upturned nose and mischievous smile, and her personality bubbled over with positivity.

She and Michaela had met in undergrad, but Michaela had studied dentistry instead of medicine. Nevertheless, their bond had stayed strong, and they were inseparable now. Michaela had joined a dental practice in Westwood. She had bought herself a condominium unit in a glossy building nearby with floor-to-ceiling glass windows. Although she made no secret of her desire to find a serious man and get married, she thoroughly enjoyed the perks of being a single professional woman living an incredible life in LA until that happened. She earnestly believed in true love and felt that her soul mate was somewhere out there, just waiting to meet her.

"I'm on the fence about what to wear," Lyra began. "I was

thinking of my red silk chiffon gown with the one-shouldered neckline."

"Oooh, that one is pretty on you," Michaela replied, and Lyra could sense the motive behind her voice. "What about that Tom Ford liquid sequin dress we found together at the Designer Sale at Nordstrom Rack? You'll glitter like a strobe light when the light hits you as you speak. It will be fantastic."

Lyra hesitated for a moment because she had actually considered wearing the fabulous sequin dress she would never have dared to purchase at full price. "Okay, but if I wear the liquid sequins, you must wear your Stella McCartney."

"Done," agreed Michaela. "I'll pick you up in the Uber at 6:00p.m., which gives us plenty of time to find our table."

"Perfect," chirped Lyra, careful to conceal the nervousness in her voice. "See you soon."

As the two women walked into the lobby of the Beverly Wilshire Hotel, they started to get excited. This was a major social event; all eyes would be on Lyra as she made her speech at the podium. Thankfully, she was due to speak after the emcee's welcoming remarks. She could relax afterward; enjoy her dinner, and whatever other surprises the evening might bring.

Helping herself to a glass of champagne offered by a circulating waiter, Michaela remarked, "Look at how marvelous the ballroom looks tonight. I'm so proud of you for giving your time and being a part of this."

"Thank you, I appreciate you for saying that," Lyra demurred, sipping her glass of bubbly. "You do your own charity work for the Smile Foundation, so I think we both give back, as we should."

"I know, but nobody has ever asked me to speak at one of

their events. You're going to be amazing." Michaela was genuinely proud of her dear friend. They had been through a lot together, and Lyra's heart was always in the right place. Looking around, she commented, "Although, I'm not sure this is the kind of party where there are any eligible bachelors. I'm trying not to be too obvious here, but as I look around, it appears to be mostly coupled."

"I'm sorry, honey," Lyra made a subtle faux pouty face. "I suspect you're right."

As they sipped their bubbly and sampled some hors d'oeuvres, they browsed the silent auction items. The long auction tables were covered with generously donated luxury items that were sure to fetch high bids. Not to mention the lavish holidays and chef's dinners on the live auction list. Lyra was pleased with the results of her committee's efforts. It was nice to know that in a world overrun by technology, people still cared enough on a personal level to make meaningful contributions to a good cause.

Sure enough, the women had been assigned to a table composed entirely of couples, except for them. When the time came for Lyra to speak, Michaela applauded enthusiastically. She watched her friend shimmy towards the podium, the lights glinting off her sequin dress. As she stepped up to the microphone, Michaela could see that Lyra was nervous by the way she reached up to finger her dangly gold earrings and tuck a wavy lock of hair behind her ear. She nodded to her friend as if to tell her she could speak now. She would be okay.

Lyra placed her speaking notes on the lectern. She began, "Ladies and gentlemen, all of us at the Smart Heart Start Society would like to earnestly thank you for your generosity in having chosen to attend our yearly fundraising gala tonight. Because of your immense support, our organization has been able to expand this year and thrive...."

"You were outstanding," Michaela whispered to her friend as they said goodnight to people on their way to the main exit to go home. "Did you hear the hush over the room while you were speaking? And those live auction items rose over $600,000.00. I think you surpassed your goal tonight."

"Well, thank you for coming and supporting me here tonight. I'm sorry it was a bust finding Mr. Right."

"I had a great time," Michaela assured her, "but I think we made the right choice to leave when the dancing started. Everyone else was obviously paired off. All these married couples...everyone is married except for us. Anyway, I just had a lovely night out with my bestie, both of us in our highest high heels. Who knows? Maybe we'll both have partners at next year's gala."

"I guess we'll see," Lyra said laughing.

The Wake-up Call

WHEN MONDAY MORNING ROLLED AROUND, Lyra was still on a high from the excitement of Saturday night's ball. How had her life become this glamorous? It seemed like only yesterday she was working as a cashier at Ralph's grocery store and tutoring on the side. Those days had seemed interminable, yet exciting at the same time because Lyra had known that she was working toward her ultimate goal of becoming a doctor. So now what? Having completed her residency and become a practicing cardiologist and an adjunct professor at UCLA, did that mean she had reached the finish line? Or was there more she needed to accomplish career-wise to feel whole?

These existential questions would have to wait because, for now, Lyra needed to wrap up her class.

"And next week, we'll talk about the risks and benefits of angioplasty and how to tell when your patient is a good candidate for that procedure. Please be sure to read chapter six and answer the questions that go with the case study. Feel free to email me if you have any questions."

The auditorium slowly emptied, with students murmuring to each another as they collected their things and left the room. After Lyra had grabbed her briefcase, she made her way up the aisle and toward an exit door. She stopped when she noticed that one of her students had fallen asleep and still had his head on his notebook, with his mouth slightly open. It was clear that he was out cold. Lyra felt sorry for him, but she had to leave and lock up the classroom.

Carefully, she nudged him awake by tapping him on the shoulder.

"Huh?" He looked up, embarrassed. "Oh, God. Don't tell me I fell asleep. Class is over. Oh my God."

"It's okay," Lyra reassured him gently.

"It's just that I worked a night shift as an orderly here at the hospital, and I thought I could come to class afterward and be fine. Clearly, I need to figure out a better sleep schedule. I'm sorry, Dr. Brunet." Her student was contrite.

"It's fine. I'll post my lecture notes online. Read chapter six for next week, and finish the questions for the case study. You'll be fine. You can catch up. We've all been there," Lyra's tone was kind and understanding.

As they left the classroom, Lyra was reminded that everyone had their challenges and that she should never get too comfortable. Thinking back, she was sure that she had never actually fallen asleep during a lecture, but she had definitely come close. Her student today must really be burning the candle at both ends. Hopefully, he would catch up and be alright. She would hate to think that someone might not have the funds to complete the program after working so hard to get into medical school.

That night after work, Lyra met Michaela at an oyster bar down at the Santa Monica Pier.

"This is totally on my diet," Michaela teased, "because

oysters are all protein, and I'm pretty sure the spicy sauce has no carbs."

"Maybe one carb in the sauce," agreed Lyra, "but I suspect our martinis are loaded with carbs."

"It's just one night, and the martinis are very dry, so they must be keto-friendly."

"Must be."

"All kidding aside, Lyra," Michaela continued, "I feel that going all out on Saturday night was an excellent thing for you —for both of us—to do. Even though everyone was married at the fundraiser, the next event might be more productive. I know that work is all-consuming for both of us, but we need to slow down and experience the joy of being human at a certain point."

"Everything you're saying is true. It's just that I don't want to date at work—that could get uncomfortable—and I feel more comfortable meeting men in person than online."

"I know," Michaela agreed. "Guys I meet online just freak me out. Looking up someone's online persona can be like going down a rabbit hole. It's not healthy."

"Right, so what do we do?" Lyra didn't have the answers either.

"According to Cosmo's Bedside Astrologer, we're supposed to be open to the universe's signs. We must pay attention, be receptive and responsive, and be willing to engage."

"Willing to engage, huh?" Lyra giggled as she took another sip of her classic martini.

"That's what I said... willing to engage."

"Alright, Michaela. You'll be the first to know."

Dante

DANTE RUSH WAS a tall drink of water, and he knew it. Not that he was egotistical, but he had grown up in the spotlight. He had made his first fortune almost entirely off his physical appearance, so he knew he was universally considered handsome. At age thirty-five, his face had lost some of its baby fat and had thinned out in a way that emphasized his high cheekbones, well-defined lips, and chiseled jawline. His body was long and leanly muscled, and since he was all legs, he looked taller than his 5'9 height. He kept his curly black hair closely cropped, and his perfectly white teeth were a beautiful contrast to his rich, chocolate-brown skin. Women also tended to admire his hands, which had elegantly long fingers and were clearly the hands of a man who hadn't done a day of manual labor. Surprisingly, this was a turn-on for many women.

His shorter height was an asset to him when he had been acting full-time because most female actors tended to be on the petite side. As soon as he finished college in the United States, he returned to France to be with his mother, a seasoned actress, until he could make more specific career plans. Luckily for him, his mother's agent found him a job as a series regular in a period drama that was being filmed on the grounds of Versailles. Immediately a fan favorite, Dante had been on the cover of every major magazine, and his role in the series grew every season, as did his paycheck. While he was on hiatus, he filmed rom-com movies in Hollywood. His film and television fame made the major fashion houses notice him. Every season, he walked the runways during Paris Fashion Week for pretty much all of the aughts.

Eventually, however, Dante realized that he was ready for a break from acting and from all the attention that it had brought him. After all the years of filming at Versailles, he had grown to love the French countryside. When the series wrapped, he decided to stay in France. As luck would have it, he purchased a château in the Burgundy region that dated back to the 14th century but had been thoroughly renovated with all modern amenities. This became his refuge, and he had no desire to return to the United States. Although he had a staff on-site to manage the estate's vineyard, he took a keen interest in winemaking and, over the years, he had developed a good sense of smell and an educated palate. His wines were very sought-after, and he felt fulfilled by this new interest.

While the pastoral setting of the château was calming and healthy in every way, living out in the country was not conducive to having an active social life. Not that he was a recluse: he had friends and traveled to Paris at least once a month. He was also dating someone, but the serial monogamist inside of him was urging him to break things off with her sooner rather than later before she got too attached.

Speaking of becoming too attached, Jaime was calling him again. In his experience, whenever he saw his girlfriend's name and number on the call display, it triggered a feeling of mild revulsion; this was his cue to end things. He allowed her call to go to voicemail and made a mental note to break up with her, face to face, before leaving for Los Angeles next week to attend his mother's Lifetime Achievement award ceremony.

Dante's mother, Araceli Rush, had made her debut in the first James Bond film. Her movie star status still eclipsed every other female in her age category, which she proudly vaunted as being over 60. Araceli had never shied away from aging, and her confidence grew commensurately with her experience. They had always enjoyed a close relationship, his father having spent most of Dante's childhood directing movies in the United States. At the same time, he and Araceli remained in France most of the time. Dante hadn't really missed him, though, since the only home he had ever known was with his mother. Araceli had never married his father, and she hadn't expressed any desire to be supported by a man. His father had eventually married the heiress to an American department store, and their relationship now consisted of sending one another holiday cards. There was little more than a biological connection. Dante had always kept his mother's surname, which suited him just fine.

Over the years, Dante had dated enough women to know what qualities were most important to him. Every one of his paramours had referred to him as being a mama's boy, and quite frankly, he found this offensive. While it may have been old-fashioned, Dante maintained a strong desire to live up to his mother's expectations of him. Above all, he wanted her to be proud of the man he had become. He prioritized his relationship with Araceli because he felt it was a mark of respect to maintain positive communication and to spend time with her as often as possible. Having Araceli approve of his girlfriends was important to him. Since he didn't have a big family, honoring his mother was a choice he was proud to make. Dante found it to be a total turnoff when women encouraged him to spend less time with his mother or to call her less often.

Unfortunately, Jaime was one of those women. She had

been offended that Dante had chosen to fly to Los Angeles for his mother's occasion instead of spending a week with her in Milan, shooting print ads for one of the big Italian fashion houses. He would have preferred Jaime to emphasize her career independence more and support his decision to attend the gala with Araceli. However, if she hadn't figured it out by now, she wouldn't get far in this relationship, and would also be jealous of the time he chose to spend with Araceli. Besides, what was Dante expected to do during her long shoot days? He wasn't the type of man to stand around and watch. Dante wasn't interested in being in the background for anyone, no matter how attractive she was and irrespective of the intensity of their sexual chemistry. He smiled wryly, thinking of a particular American pop star that would have referred to Jaime as "sexual napalm." Perhaps after they broke up, she could go and find that singer and inspire his next studio album.

The only unfortunate thing about Dante's serial monogamy was that the pattern wasn't conducive to becoming engaged, married, and finally starting a family. Now that he was in his mid-thirties, he was beginning to feel a touch of hunger, a little bit of longing, and that biological urge to pair up and start a family. Now that Araceli had reached all of her career milestones and could choose her film projects, she was also becoming more vocal about her desire to see her son get married. After all, she wanted to be a healthy and active young grandmother. Dante was confident that he would find the right partner at some point, but he was also sure Jaime wasn't the right person to fulfill that role. Araceli would have to wait just a bit longer before she could call herself the mother of the groom.

Moments later, his phone rang a second time, and he answered as soon as he saw Araceli's name on the screen.

"Allo, Maman," he began.

"Mon Cher," cooed Araceli in her trademark bedtime story voice. "I want to make sure that you're still planning to accompany me to Los Angeles next week to attend my award ceremony?"

"Of course, Maman, you know I wouldn't miss the opportunity to walk a red carpet with you. Everything has been coordinated: our flights, hotel, and wardrobe."

"Thank you, my boy. I'm so fortunate to have such a reliable and attentive son. I'll see you soon."

Adieu

ALWAYS ON THE lookout for another real estate deal, Dante couldn't resist when an opportunity arose last month in Brussels. Even though this deal threatened to cut into some of his time in Los Angeles with his mother, he knew that buying this commercial property was a major coup. He had already done his due diligence and lined up the appropriate financing, concerning the purchase of this boutique hotel in Brussels. Still, he hadn't expected everything to come together so quickly. Nevertheless, if he flew to Belgium tomorrow, he would still make it to Los Angeles with plenty of time to prepare for and attend his mother's event.

Damn, he thought to himself. This meant that if he wanted to free himself of the albatross around his neck that was Jaime, he would have to do it immediately. These women always behaved so tragically when he broke up with them. He found it pathetic that after just a few dates, they fashioned their entire lives around his schedule, and they seemed to want to ingratiate themselves into every aspect of his life. He knew that he was handsome and keenly aware of how attractive women found his vast wealth to be. Still, at the same time, he kept expecting to be able to pursue an actual healthy and reciprocal relationship. What would it take for him to get there? Weren't there any women out there who put themselves and their careers first anymore? He didn't want to date a bitch, but he definitely wanted to find someone who valued herself, her own goals, and her career ambitions above all else.

One thing was sure: Dante did not want to think about Jaime while trying to enjoy himself in Los Angeles. He would have to cut the cord sooner rather than later. To this end, Dante asked his staff to prepare a candlelit dinner for two in the courtyard. He invited Jaime to come over that evening for dinner at 8:00p.m. In anticipation of their breakup, he also asked his personal butler to comb through his bedroom drawers. Every shelf in his master ensuite, as well as any coat or shoe closets, so that he could collect all of Jaime's belongings and pack them up before her arrival. He didn't want her to find any excuse to return after he had pulled the plug on their romance. When Dante was done, he was done, and there was no going back.

Jaime arrived promptly at 8:00p.m. Dante watched from the window as her long, lean legs exited her Porsche Boxter convertible at an angle before she lifted her body out of the driver's seat. Her long, shiny blonde hair shimmered in the moonlight. God, she was gorgeous, Dante thought to himself. Gorgeous but vapid. He had a weakness for models, perhaps because his mother had been a runway model before she broke into film, so there was potentially a hint of the Oedipus Complex.

Nevertheless, he had to follow through with the breakup because although their sexual chemistry was positively combustible, that's all there was. He had looked at this relationship with an analytical eye. There was no long-term potential, no chance that he would ever want to marry this woman and build a family with her. Something inside of him was telling him that Jaime wasn't the one.

Even her walk was sexy, he noticed, as he watched her sashay along the path that led to his massive 14th-century front doors. Her pale blue sequin mini dress sparkled as the light from his lamp posts refracted from it. When he greeted her at the door, he felt that her emerald green eyes were almost cat-like in the near-darkness. Jaime was one inch taller than him, which hadn't bothered him since everything evened out when they were lying in bed. In her stiletto heels tonight, she seemed to tower over him. Her stature made it seem like she was more of a caricature than a living, breathing human being, which may have contributed to his treating her as if she was expendable.

Dante kissed her cheek as he led her inside, and he couldn't help but be turned on just a little bit by her trademark perfume: Lost Cherry by Tom Ford. Jaime had just completed a two-year exclusive contract with the brand for beauty and fashion. She was now free to walk again at all the major metropolitan fashion shows. All the prominent designers were clamoring for Jaime to walk for them next season. Dante had no doubt that she would recover from their breakup. Her ego would be bruised, but he had no doubt that she would land herself another wealthy man at Paris Fashion Week or maybe London's. In any event, Dante knew that he had treated her well while they were together. It would be cruel to keep her hanging on when he had already decided that he was ready to dispose of her.

They dined on fennel and orange salad, followed by filet mignon with potatoes and asparagus. Dante ordered a burgundy from his vineyard to drink that night, along with sparkling water. They made the usual small talk throughout dinner, and when the espresso and sorbet arrived, Dante dropped his bomb.

"Jaime," he began, "our time together has been charming, and now it must end. I've enjoyed getting to know you immensely, but I just don't see a long-term future for us, and as a result, it's time for us to part ways."

For a moment, she didn't speak. Her lips trembled, and Dante was worried that she might cry, which he detested. However, Jaime didn't shed a tear. She appeared to be considering her words carefully.

"I'm shocked. I don't understand where this is coming from. I thought you would invite me to Los Angeles on your trip with your mother." Something in Jaime's eyes told Dante that she wasn't going to accept defeat as easily as he had hoped.

"You're obviously a stunningly beautiful woman," he reassured her. "I know that you'll be in another relationship in no time. It won't be difficult for you to find someone new."

"I don't want to find a new man, Dante. I only want to be with you. I feel shocked at this moment and betrayed. I've never had chemistry with any man the way I have with you, and I highly doubt that you will find another woman who can make love to you the way I do and who will be as loyal to you as I am."

"I understand that you're upset," he conceded. "Yes, our chemistry is off the charts. Unfortunately, I just don't see us going the distance together. Our dating time has been fun, but Jaime, what we have together is just too casual for me. I don't feel as invested emotionally as you deserve. I'm sorry."

"Yes," she said as she got up from her chair. "I believe you'll miss me, and you will be sorry." Jaime felt utterly humiliated. Looking around, she noticed Dante's butler standing near the entryway. He coolly held what appeared to be a soft-sided suitcase. Jaime presumed it to be full of her toiletries and other small belongings that she had left at his house for her convenience whenever she spent the night. She realized that

Dante had been planning to break up with her for quite some time, seeing as he could direct his staff to collect her things.

With those words, she stalked toward the front door, where Dante's butler handed her the bag filled with her belongings. She turned to give Dante one last, rueful look as she took the bag and walked out the imposing front door and into the warm night. He didn't look out the window to watch her get into her car and drive away. Oh well, he thought to himself, easy come, easy go. At least he had only taken up a few months of her time.

Two Worlds Colliding

FINALLY, after he had managed to shake off the guilt surrounding his break-up with Jaime, Dante went to Brussels and successfully purchased the boutique hotel in person. After that, he flew directly to Los Angeles, where he booked Bungalow 5 at the Beverly Hills Hotel for himself and his mother to stay. He knew she had been friends with the late Elizabeth Taylor, who had taken up residence in this bungalow for a while. With all of her industry experience and generous heart, Liz had been a true mentor to Araceli, taken her under her wing, and protected her. Liz had introduced her to the most influential directors in Hollywood and throughout Europe. This had created significant opportunities for Araceli, for which she would always be grateful. In fact, the influence of the fabulous Liz Taylor led Araceli to the success and fame she is experiencing today.

Earning a Lifetime Achievement Award was perhaps Araceli's crowning career accomplishment, and her son wanted to make everything about this occasion extra special. After all, no one else in her life was as devoted to her as he was, and it pleased him to see her dreams come true. Although she had never revealed it, Dante had heard from other sources that Araceli had turned down numerous movie roles. At the same time, he was quite young, so she might remain as present as possible for her child when he needed her. Going all out for her big awards ceremony was the least he could do to demonstrate his appreciation for all his mother had done and continued to do for him. Araceli had a strong moral compass, and she was his guiding light. Dante's mission was to live up to his mother's expectations.

Preparations for the event were a lot of fun. They dined on crudités and canapés in their bungalow as the hairstylist and makeup artist had flitted all about Araceli, who was all the while wearing a luxurious pink silk robe. Then, while Dante was getting into his midnight blue suit, the stylist helped Araceli put on a glamorous evening gown in a coordinating shade of blue. As he beheld his mother before they left, he felt she looked regal. He was so full of admiration for her and for all she had accomplished as an unmarried black female actress. She was definitely a force to be reckoned with.

A limousine picked them up at the hotel and delivered them to the Dolby Theater, where they walked the red carpet together. Dante was used to the drill and had become quite good at it over the years, even though he had left his glitzy Hollywood life behind. The feeling of having all eyes on him, combined with the constant clicking of the paparazzi cameras, was intoxicating. He reveled in the attention while deferring to his mother as he followed her lead. She smiled her radiant smile in all directions, allowing the photographers to capture all her best angles. She gave short interviews with entertainment news reporters. Araceli found it thrilling that, even beyond age 60, Hollywood recognized her worth as an actress. She hoped that this new pro-age way of thinking would endure, that it wasn't just a passing trend.

Once inside the auditorium, they settled in their seats and

visited with many familiar friends from the industry. Dante was elated when it was Araceli's turn to receive her award. She gave an elegant thank you speech, allowing herself to shed only a few tears of appreciation so as not to ruin her makeup. The applause was deafening. This was Araceli's moment, and she indulged herself with a few extra seconds at the podium to breathe and take it all in.

As she was making her way back to her seat, Dante noticed that she seemed to be slightly unsure of her footing. When he saw that she was suddenly covered in a layer of perspiration, he knew that her four-inch heels weren't the culprit. He stood up as she approached their aisle, holding her hand to help steady her footing. Suddenly, Araceli went limp. She collapsed heavily onto the thick velvet pile carpet, the award rolling out of her hand and traveling downward before finally coming to rest at the edge of the stage. Fortunately, Dante had succeeded in half-catching her, preventing her head from hitting the floor first.

"Somebody, call 911! We need an ambulance," there was no mistaking the urgency in Dante's voice. Within minutes, the EMTs arrived and placed Araceli onto a stretcher. He rode with her in the ambulance to the Ronald Reagan Medical Center.

Lyra had just experienced what could possibly have been the most successful day of her medical career to date. A beloved sitcom actor starring in a successful television series had been feeling unwell on set. He had been experiencing severe nausea and was transported to the hospital under suspicion of food poisoning. Luckily, Lyra had been called in to examine him when the emergency room team detected an irregular heartbeat. As soon as she noticed he was paper-white pale and he

27

had a gray tinge to his face, she ordered an ultrasound of his heart. Thankfully, the images detected a tear in his aorta. Before things worsened, the patient was brought in for an emergency surgery, the tear was repaired, and the crisis was averted.

Lyra was congratulated by her Chief of Staff when she heard herself being paged to return to the ER to meet another patient who had just arrived by ambulance. Completely exhausted, Lyra took a moment to collect herself. She reminded herself of how much she loved her career and how meaningful it was to her to be in a position to help people. After a few deep, grounding breaths, Lyra was ready for another round. She felt completely spent from the weight of the cognitive load from dealing with her last patient. Still, clearly, someone else needed her medical attention now. She would get through this next case on adrenaline if she had to, and she would rest later.

She walked quickly to the emergency ward, where she could see and hear quite a lot of commotion surrounding the new patient that had just arrived by ambulance. In her peripheral vision, she could make out at least a dozen paparazzi taking photos through the windows with their giant flash cameras. The noise the crowd of onlookers created on the other side of the glass added to the hospital's stress level. Lyra asked the head nurse to summon security and remove the reporters and photographers. She wondered who this patient could be and who was attracting such media attention. It must be someone even more famous than her previous patient.

That's when Lyra saw her—Araceli Rush—being wheeled in from the ambulance. Although her face was partially obstructed by an oxygen mask, her regal hairline and profile were distinctly recognizable. Lyra had taken a few minutes earlier to read the People website while eating her lunch that afternoon. She had read about Araceli being in town to receive a Lifetime Achievement Award from the Academy. It must be her. Lyra had never dreamed that she would meet her favorite actress. Her heart fluttered nervously at the thought that now she would be responsible for stabilizing her condition. She knew she needed to focus and call upon all her knowledge because she couldn't afford to make any mistakes with this precious patient. She was experienced enough to know that no one was ever supposed to get special treatment. Still, she couldn't help but feel extra determined to see Araceli restored to perfect health.

As soon as Araceli was wheeled into a room, Lyra reviewed her vitals and all the notes made by the ambulance staff. She completed her initial assessment of her patient, and then ordered the full complement of tests to be conducted upon Araceli, post-haste. Still unconscious on the stretcher, Araceli was wheeled back into the cardiology unit. Here the nurses and technicians completed everything from an electrocardiogram to an MRI and everything in between. Throughout this time, Lyra reviewed Araceli's test results online and made notes for herself. It was quite concerning to her that her patient had still not regained consciousness. She called the cardiac surgeon on-call to discuss possible courses of action and expected outcomes.

That's when she saw him: Dante Rush, in the flesh. She remembered him when he starred in that period drama set in a castle. Ding dong, she thought to herself, was he ever gorgeous. Then Lyra shook her head and directed her mind back to the case. She wouldn't let Dante's handsome face cloud her ability to diagnose and treat a patient.

"Would you please have someone send a doctor to speak to me?" Dante's voice was clipped more than it needed to be, and his curt tone surprised Lyra. She was well-accustomed to communicating with patient families, often in worse circumstances than Araceli Rush's. Nobody had ever spoken to her so rudely. She was doing the best she could.

"I'm the cardiologist on shift here. My name is Dr. Lyra Brunet, and may I presume you're the patient's son?" she attempted to change the tone of their dialogue.

"I'm sorry, miss, but I think you're mistaken," he practically spat the words out at her. "I expect a senior cardiologist to treat my mother, not some lowly intern. I'll pay the extra fee for a qualified physician."

Trying her best to remain professional, Lyra replied, "I understand you're going through a lot right now, Mr. Rush, but I assure you that I'm qualified to take on your mother's case. Please allow me a few minutes to review her test results, and then I'll come back to you and discuss our best course of action."

Dante turned on his heel and walked briskly toward the nursing station. She could see him gesticulating impatiently. Lyra overheard him demand the attention of a qualified cardiologist instead of some baby sorority girl. Lyra had witnessed a lot in her years at the hospital, but until now, she hadn't seen a full-on temper tantrum by a grown man who should know better. She would have laughed at him if she hadn't been so intently focused on solving Araceli's cardiac crisis.

The Widowmaker

AFTER WHAT SEEMED LIKE FOREVER, but only a few minutes, the orderlies wheeled Araceli into an operating room prepared for her. She was stable enough to proceed with corrective surgery. Dante had been on his mobile phone the whole time. Pacing back and forth, he called California's top cardiologists, asking them to fly in by helicopter to tend to Araceli. He wasn't happy that each of them assured him that Dr. Lyra Brunet was top-notch and that she would provide the best medical care to his beloved mother. This response seemed to have angered Dante further. Now he was slightly embarrassed at his childlike behavior, and he would have to eat crow to get into Lyra's good graces. Luckily for him, Lyra wasn't petty, and she didn't care to hold grudges, so for her, it was business as usual... and Lyra was in the business of saving lives.

Putting Dante's infantile—and quite frankly, insulting—behavior out of her mind, Lyra assembled her team. She consulted with the cardiac surgeon who would be handling Araceli's case. Luckily, Dr. Theo Saunders was the cardiac surgeon on shift that evening. He grew up in an Italian New Jersey family, and his no-nonsense attitude enabled him to assess urgent situations calmly and clearly. Theo and Lyra had completed part of their residencies and were good work friends. Theo was engaged to marry Rowan, a brilliant registered nurse who also happened to work on their unit.

Since they had such a good rapport, Theo and Lyra could practically finish one another's sentences. They were so in sync professionally that they could quickly diagnose Araceli's problem. Together, they determined that angioplasty and stenting would be the most prudent plan, with the best long-term outcome in this patient. After several hours of surgery, Lyra was completely spent. Still, she gathered up her strength in anticipation of providing an explanation to Dante that would likely trigger an oppositional reaction. She had to steel herself in anticipation of his misplaced criticism.

"Please tell me what happened to my mother," Dante said contritely. The nurses had been watching him pace up and down the hallways for the duration of his mother's surgery. "I'm very concerned. She was fine all day. We were laughing, enjoying ourselves, and she didn't complain of any chest pains, nausea, or headache. Nothing. She was her usual self. It was just a sudden collapse, so completely unexpected, and her demeanor changed instantly, without any warning."

"I understand you're in shock and traumatized, and you're worried about your mother. This is normal and healthy," Lyra reassured him. "From what I can tell, Araceli experienced a massive heart attack. I can see from her medical records that she has previously had no health issues. She's young, fit, and an appropriate weight for her height. She doesn't smoke, nor does she drink excessively. There is also no history of drug use, not even a prescription. This is a highly unusual scenario. With everything else about her in good working order, she will have an excellent prognosis with the right care."

"So what are you saying?" Dante asked impatiently.

"Mr. Rush, your mother suffered what has come to be

colloquially known as a 'widowmaker' heart attack. The name belies that women are just as often victims as men. In women, the warning signs of this particular kind of heart attack are so subtle that it's easy to miss them, which is part of what makes the widowmaker so deadly. Did you happen to notice whether Araceli exhibited neck or jaw pain, nausea, or lightheadedness earlier in the day? Or any type of cold sweats?"

"No, she was just in a glorious, upbeat mood. If anything was off, she didn't share that with me."

"Well, as you know," Lyra continued, "there are many kinds of heart attacks. In Araceli's case, plaque blockage formed in the left anterior descending artery. This artery supplies blood to the larger front part of the heart; in her case, the LAD artery showed a blockage at its origin. When a person is experiencing a heart attack, every minute matters. The longer certain parts of the heart are deprived of blood and oxygen, the more the heart muscle will be damaged. Luckily, the emergency team in the ambulance was able to administer some clot-dissolving medication en route to the hospital, which improved her prognosis.

"Once Araceli was admitted here, our team could locate the precise placement of the blockage and take it from there to clear the obstruction. We opted to treat your mother using angioplasty and stenting, which seems to have done the trick. Araceli's medical history shows she is resilient and will recover nicely, provided she avoids stressful activities and she allows herself the appropriate time for recovery. Within a few months, we can examine her again, give her the all-clear for travel, and resume her normal work and leisure schedule. Does that sound fair to you? Do you have any questions?"

"When can I see her?" Dante asked anxiously. "Is she awake?"

"I'm afraid your mother is still in recovery. You'll have to wait until she is stable before you start asking her questions,"

Lyra spoke sternly to Dante. "She's about to be admitted to my cardiology unit, so we'll give you a room number as soon as one is assigned. I prefer you to just sit with her calmly, hold her hand for comfort, and let her know that you're there with her. However, please don't try and make her speak or cause her any stress. Just be present, and keep calm."

"I understand," was all he said. Not that she needed or expected any kind of apology or thank you from him. Still, after his petulant behavior, Lyra would have thought that Dante might have somehow acknowledged that she had succeeded in capably treating Araceli. Some people are just really full of themselves, she thought to herself as she walked away. Finally clocking out, she could go home, take a nice, hot shower, and put herself mercifully to bed.

Mama's Boy

AS SHE WOKE up the next morning, Lyra looked back on the crazy day that was yesterday. She had treated two major celebrities on the same day. It had been months since anyone interesting had crossed her path at work, and the previous day had practically been an embarrassment of riches. Before bed last night, she had texted Michaela to let her know of the events of the day. As she fell asleep in bed, she saw that Araceli's story had made the national news headlines. Thank goodness everything had worked out the way it did. She wouldn't have been able to forgive herself if she had made a mistake with Araceli, and neither would her son. She was sure he would be the type to file a malpractice suit the moment a doctor did something he didn't like. As handsome as he was, Lyra felt that Dante had ruined her day yesterday. His shocking behavior towards her in the hospital had needlessly raised her stress levels. He was a real jerk.

Even though Lyra wanted to despise Dante, she couldn't help but be curious about him. Who was this guy? Against her better judgment, she found herself going down the rabbit hole that was Google. Obviously, he was involved in some kind of acting and modeling career because his features were too symmetrical for him to be a normal man. Moreover, his ego was so huge that she felt he must either be a big shot producer or he had followed in his mother's footsteps and acted in Europe, where she may not have seen anything he was in.

Her online search immediately yielded the results she had anticipated: Dante had starred in a major television series about ten years ago. Right when his fame was at its height, Lyra would have been studying like a madwoman to get accepted into medical school. For several years, she barely watched television and rarely went out to see any movies. She had her nose in a book for over a decade, so it took her a minute to recognize Dante.

According to online sources, once his big period drama had wrapped production, Dante shifted gears and started investing in real estate. He was a significant investor in commercial retail and hotel properties all over Europe. His most recent venture was commercial vineyards. For the past few years, Dante had been scooping up family-owned wineries in Italy and France, overseeing the production of several biodynamic wines. This was a growing trend, with the biodynamic label being more highly prized than simply an organic denomination.

On the personal side, the internet described him as never having been married. In the images section are hundreds of photos of Dante with gorgeous women, mostly tall and glamorous. The one constant was that he was frequently photographed at events with his mother. Out for dinner or shopping with her. The tabloids described him as a mama's boy and a model-izer. He had a penchant for hanging out with his mom and a reputation for only dating models. No wonder he behaved like such a jackass, Lyra thought to herself. I must be too insignificant to warrant his admiration and respect. The web painted Dante as some kind of wealthy international playboy, a man of mystery, the scion of one of Hollywood's grand dames. He had been born with a silver spoon in his mouth, and he had used that advantage to take his financial success to new heights.

Above all, Lyra had determined that Dante was a pompous ass. Nevertheless, she couldn't shake the thoughts of his face from her head. Something about him intrigued her, and she was embarrassed to let her mind go there. Of all the men she could find herself attracted to—however minimally, contradictorily—why did it have to be this colossal jerk? She shook her head, finished eating her breakfast of overnight oats with apples, cinnamon, chia seeds, and maple syrup, and went upstairs to prepare for another day at work.

Turning Point

LATER THAT DAY, Lyra checked on Araceli as soon as she began her rounds. She found it a bit intimidating that Dante was always on top of the nursing staff, demanding some explanation every hour. She had received reports from her team that he was unnecessarily rude to everyone. All the nurses and attendant physicians were doing everything they could to keep his mother comfortable. Checking and recording her vitals and doing their jobs to the best of their abilities. Dante's interference was more of a hindrance than help.

When she saw Araceli, it was evident that she wasn't recovering from her massive heart attack quite as quickly as everyone had hoped. She could breathe independently but was still weak and unable to talk. Out of an abundance of caution, Lyra instructed that her oxygen mask be kept on. There must be more significant damage to her heart than they had initially thought. Nevertheless, the angioplasty and stent were doing their jobs, and her blood flow and heartbeat were consistent and regular. The blood thinning medication seemed to be keeping any further clots at bay. Lyra believed her patient would recover, but it might take longer than anticipated.

Wanting to avoid crossing paths with Dante, Lyra made sure to enter very detailed notes on Araceli's condition into the hospital's system. This way, her nursing staff and any other doctors on shift could give Dante an update. She found his manner quite off-putting. She felt that she had taken enough of a verbal beating from him yesterday that she didn't need to place herself in the line of fire again today. Hopefully, he would be reassured of his mother's positive prognosis and mellow out just a little bit.

Thankfully, Lyra spotted Theo in the hallway having an intense-looking discussion with Dante, presumably about Araceli's predicted recovery. Instead of continuing on her path, Lyra returned around the corner because she didn't want to join the conversation. After all, Theo was a male cardiac surgeon and, therefore, more credible in Dante's eyes than she would ever be. Maybe hearing a man explain things would finally put Dante at ease, at least to the point where he wouldn't belittle the hospital staff. You would think that a celebrity would at least pretend to be nice, she thought to herself, for reputation's sake. He looked completely disheveled, as though he had slept in the visitor's chair in his mother's room the night before. Truth be told, Lyra felt a little bit sorry for him.

When Dante finally left the hospital, presumably to return to his hotel to eat, rest, and freshen up, Lyra went in to check on Araceli again. Her vitals were all stable. Lyra figured that she probably needed another day or two of recovery before they could remove the oxygen mask, do more exams, and start thinking about rehabilitation.

"Hey, Lyra," she heard Theo's voice come up behind her. "Let's go get a coffee. We'll update one another on all our famous patients."

"You got it, I could use a break, and you can bring me up to speed on your wedding plans."

"That's all in Rowan's capable hands," he said jokingly. "Seriously, if you can picture two big Italian families coming together for a wedding, it's safe to say that it won't be low-key. We'll be vibrating for weeks after all that excitement."

"Sounds like fun," Lyra replied with a laugh. "I look forward to it."

"Speaking of weddings," Theo began, "It's been years—actually years—since I've seen you date anyone. Have you ever asked yourself what you're really looking for, Lyra? I mean, you have this career, you have the house, you're beautiful, and you're smart. Please explain to me how you're still single."

"Theo, where were you last night? If I had to guess, I'd say you slept in the call room. How do you think men handle it when I have to cancel my dates because an ambulance brought in another cardiac patient at the end of my shift? Men don't like to come second, and I don't have to tell you that my medical career will always take priority."

"You know what I think?" Theo began. "I think we need to introduce you to a confident, charismatic man of substance who isn't intimidated by your level of career success."

"You know I'm always open to that, Theo," she said lightly. "However, something tells me that your next assertion will be that Mr. Right is right under my nose, and I just haven't recognized him yet." Her friend laughed gently.

Lyra was glad that Theo hadn't picked up on the tension she was feeling surrounding Dante. The last thing she needed was for Theo to find excuses for her to contact Dante to update him on his mother's condition. She would keep avoiding speaking to him face-to-face if possible. Lyra was starting to feel nervous about speaking to Dante again, which was highly unusual for her. Usually, Lyra could handle talking to anyone, and she had always maintained an emotional distance from her patients and their families because that's what they taught in medical school. So why was she having such a hard time wrapping her mind around the whole Dante situation?

On top of that, why was she letting thoughts about Dante take up so much of her mind? Even his physique was just right: not too tall, but tall enough. Not too slim, but slim enough, not too muscular, and just toned. She shook her head as if to clear it, but images of Dante's perfect face reappeared in her mind; she just couldn't shake him, no matter how hard she tried.

The Fantasy

"Ms. Rush, I'm pleased to let you know that, while you're not quite stable enough to be discharged, I can safely say that you've turned the corner. Your most recent test results give me a reason to believe that, with the appropriate amount of rest, you will soon be able to ease yourself back into your normal routine and eventually make a full recovery."

Lyra finally delivered some good news to her formerly critically ill patient. A few more days had gone by, and although she wasn't up and walking yet, Araceli had started speaking again—in a more muted and uncertain voice. Still, she was strong enough to start communicating a little bit. She still had no appetite and was on intravenous support, but her oxygen saturation levels were finally more consistent. Ultrasounds revealed that the damage caused to her heart was minimal; thanks mainly to Lyra's intervention, so there appeared to be very little scar tissue.

"Thank you, Dr. Brunet," Araceli whispered. "You have been my guardian angel. I'm so fortunate that you were my doctor when the ambulance brought me here. I hope my son has given you the praise you are due."

"Oh, I'm just doing my job, Ms. Rush. I don't need praise from anyone. All I need now is for you to get better so that I can send you home," Lyra's mother had taught her to always be humble, which was a valuable lesson. She had hoped that she could be in and out of Araceli's room before Dante came in that morning, but of course, he chose this moment to arrive.

"Yes, Maman," Dante lied. "Of course, from the start, I had full confidence in Dr. Brunet's ability to bring you back to your usual vibrant self." Lyra couldn't help but make a bit of a choking sound when she heard Dante utter this blatant lie.

"My son is so wonderful," Araceli's soft voice seemed to perk up a bit now that her son had returned. "I was so scared because as I passed out, I felt like that was the end. I thought to myself, please God, let me live so I can see my beautiful son find the woman of his dreams and marry. All I have ever wanted was to see my Dante married, settled down, and happily raising a loving family."

"Well, I'm content to reassure you that you will be able to experience all that joy, and I'm willing to bet that it will all happen very soon. You won't be missing out on anything." Lyra couldn't help but smile at this wonderful woman who had no idea what a rude jerk her son actually was. She wondered how it was even possible that this sweet, unassuming, soft-spoken woman was the mother of such a bore.

"Yes, Maman," Dante interjected awkwardly. "You mustn't speak as though you're at death's door. Thanks to Dr. Brunet, you'll recover fully, but it will take some time. In fact, we might one day consider your heart attack a blessing, for it has led me to my one true love."

At this point, Lyra's mouth was slightly open, and she turned her head to stare at him. What on earth was he talking about? If she didn't know better, she would think he'd just had a lobotomy because he was acting like a completely different person. It was as if Dante the cad had been replaced by a teenage boy, desperately trying to show his mommy how good he was. Was she suddenly in The Twilight Zone?

"What's this I hear?" Araceli's voice seemed to have a bit of a lilt to it now. "Is there some important news about your love life that you need to tell me?"

Dante had pulled up the visitor's chair to his mother's bedside so he could sit near her face and hold her hand as he spoke to her. "Maman, you are going to say that this sounds like a fairy tale, too good to be true, but I swear to you that what I'm telling you is the biggest miracle we could ever have wished for."

Lyra stood there silently. She had completed her exam, so technically, she could have left the room, but something inside her told her that she might want to hear what Dante was about to say. Lyra was obviously aware of his acting abilities, and she thought she might be witnessing the pilot episode for a new medical drama. She couldn't wait to hear the baloney that was about to come out of his mouth.

"Maman, when you had your heart attack and we brought you here by ambulance, my whole world started to fall apart. You are everything to me, and I was terrified of losing you. My hope was renewed as soon as the paramedics wheeled you into the hospital. You were so fortunate that the absolute best cardiologist in California happened to be working the night of the awards show. As I watched her examine you, order the necessary tests, and give instructions to the people working with her, I knew that this brilliant doctor would save your life."

"As I observed her demeanor, ability to take charge of the situation, and demonstration of knowledge and gentle patient care, I became completely intrigued. Who was this creature, and how did we get so fortunate as to have her come into our

45

lives? Maman, the person I'm speaking of is Lyra Brunet, your beautiful doctor."

If Lyra were a computer chip, her icon would have still been turning around in circles because she wasn't processing what was happening. It sounded like Dante was going off on some dramatic tangent, and she didn't know where it was headed, but his tale was fascinating in the oddest way. Half of her was dying to hear what he had to say next, and the other half was terrified because she was starting to sense where he was going with his story, and she didn't think she liked it. But she was completely frozen.

"Maman," continued Dante, in a voice so impassioned it could have passed for desperate. "After your surgery, when Lyra came to report back to me that you were going to recover, I saw something in her eyes that I've never seen before. A depth of spirit, compassion, and character. That's when I knew, Maman, that Lyra was the woman for me."

Lyra just stood there, immobile. She wanted to say something, to object to the insanity of the words that were spewing from Dante's mouth. Still, she felt like she was in a dream, being chased by a monster, trying to scream for help but unable to open her mouth to make the scream come out. Since when does he call me Lyra? She thought to herself. How does he even know my first name? This is ridiculous.

For her part, Araceli had an unprecedented look of utter joy and elation spreading across her face as she looked expectantly from Dante to Lyra, then back again.

"I know what you're thinking, Maman. You're asking yourself, how could my son have fallen so deeply in love in such a short time? You've only been in the hospital for a week. The simple fact is that women like Lyra don't come around every day. From the moment we first spoke, from our first touch, I could sense that this was the woman that I wanted to make my whole life with. She's agreed to marry me and make me the happiest man alive for two reasons: one, she saved your life, and two, her love has opened me up to a new life that I had never imagined."

"As soon as you've fully recovered, Lyra will seek your help to plan the perfect wedding. Either here in Los Angeles, or at home in France, at my—excuse me, our—château," he said, looking at Lyra for emphasis.

"Why not have two ceremonies?" Araceli seemed very pleased. "We could first have a wedding here in Los Angeles for Lyra. Then we could host a second reception in France for our friends and family to come and celebrate your union. Oh, I'm so happy. I'm so grateful you've taken such good care of me here, my dear Lyra. I could not have wished for better. This is truly a day of miracles."

Appearances

IT WAS as if Lyra couldn't get out of Araceli's hospital room quickly enough. Once she was safely out the door and out of earshot, Dante caught up with her. The look on his face told her he knew he'd done something dangerous, yet it was as if he didn't care. What kind of person makes up that kind of lie? Did the man have no scruples?

"Wait," he said, his tone pleading. "I know what you're thinking. I'm fully aware that I acted like an asshole before. However, as you can see, my mother is finally recuperating. She's on a good path, and all she's ever wanted was to see me fall in love, get married, and get settled. I'm begging you; just let her believe that we're together and getting married so that she continues on her path to recovery."

"Yes, Mr. Rush, you are a complete and utter asshole. To say the least. How dare you put me in this position? You don't even know me. You know nothing about me or how your little charade could impact my life."

"You should probably call me Dante since we're getting married," his tone was light, and God help her. Lyra couldn't stop her lips from curving into just the tiniest smile.

"Dante, you are a complete jackass. I don't know what I'm going to do with you."

"I could think of a few things," he replied suggestively.

"Are you kidding me right now?"

"Look," he continued, "I know I'm asking a lot of you. I promise I'll behave from now on. Please, please, just go along with this engagement story until my mother is fully in the clear and it's medically safe for her to fly back to Paris. I promise to make a very generous donation to a charity of your choice, so we can think of this as a philanthropic act. It can be a win-win. Please."

Lyra was in no way prepared for this. She had never imagined being put in an impossible situation like this. Who did this guy think he was? The reality was that Araceli had suffered a massive heart attack a week ago and Lyra had somehow managed to bring her back from the brink of death. If she were to pull the rug out from under her now and tell her that Dante's love story was a total farce, the shock of that unhappy news could potentially trigger another cardiac event for Araceli. That was the last thing Lyra wanted.

"Fine," she said matter-of-factly. "I'm going to ask you to pledge $250,000.00 to the Smart Heart Start Society. That will buy you a few weeks of gratitude and cooperation from me. As soon as I determine that your mother is medically well enough to hear some disappointing news, you need to promise me that you'll come clean. No more drama."

"I will. It's a deal." Dante breathed a sigh of relief.

As Lyra looked at him, she began understanding where he had gotten this sense of entitlement. He was really ridiculously good-looking, and he was charming too. As much as she wanted to hate him, there was an innocence to Dante that Lyra found endearing. She didn't want to admit it, but she couldn't stop thinking about him. Now that they had a fake relationship, she had a legitimate excuse to think about him.

Michaela would tell her that she should view this as an opportunity because you can never tell what will happen. If she were being honest with herself, she would have to admit that even with all the warning bells going off inside her head, there was something irresistible about him.

"Michaela," Lyra had snuck away to her office the first chance she got. She was dying to talk to her best friend about her fake engagement. After all, how often was it that the half-famous son of a mega-movie star asked her on a date, let alone asked for her hand in mock matrimony? This was enormous news, and she was dying to tell someone about it. As annoyed as she was, she couldn't help but feel flattered and just a tiny bit excited. As far back as she could remember, she had never been pursued by anyone as rich, famous, or charming as him. She wondered if there could be a potential downside to this. Would Araceli be upset, or take a turn for the worse, health-wise, when the jig was up?

"Hi, hon. I'm just on a break between patients. What's up? Do you want to go for a run tonight in the canyon?"

"I have news. As in major news," Lyra didn't know exactly what she could tell her friend. She didn't want the tabloids to pick up on anything. Lyra was keenly aware of their presence outside the perimeter of the hospital every single day as she came and left work.

"What kind of news? Did you find Chanel shoes on sale or something?" Michaela loved shopping almost as much as she loved dating.

"I'm engaged. Well, sort of engaged, but you have to keep it a total secret. I mean it, please. Can I trust you?" Lyra asked her friend.

"Yes, yes, of course, I'll keep anything a secret for you,"

Michaela reassured her. "But how could you get engaged, and why would it be a secret?"

"Because it's not real."

"I'm not following," Michaela said, obviously confused.

"Okay, I'll back up. You know how Araceli Rush had that massive heart attack last week in the middle of the big Hollywood awards show?"

"Yes, you saved the life of a major motion picture star. It was a huge deal. And this is connected to your engagement. How?"

"Her son, Dante Rush," Lyra began.

"Super hot. Major. Incredibly, on fire, incendiary, and a man of mystery...."

"It's him," Lyra breathed.

"No! But you didn't even tell me you were dating!"

"We're not. It's not real. We haven't even kissed," Lyra started to explain.

"You haven't kissed, you're not dating, and you're engaged, but it's not real." Michaela's voice betrayed her skepticism.

"Okay," Lyra continued, realizing how bizarre her story sounded as the words came tumbling out her mouth. "So Araceli just regained her ability to speak. She's starting to show signs of recovery. Dante sat at her bedside and told her that her greatest wish had come true, that he's met the woman of his dreams, and that we're getting married."

"Well, I guess this is where I congratulate you. Don't get me wrong, I'm really excited to hear this news, and I'm happy for you if you're happy. You just sound confused at the moment," Michaela let her words come out cautiously.

"I know. I don't know what to say, either, or what to feel. This is all just beyond my comprehension, and I'm not sure what I'm supposed to be doing. Please keep this news under wraps until we speak further?"

"Of course. I love you, honey. Chat tonight?"

"Yes, and thank you, Michaela."

In certain regards, Dante was so spoiled that he was used to behaving impetuously and then having someone else pick up the pieces. This wasn't necessarily true for his business dealings. Still, he tended to act first and think later in matters relating to women. He may be a very astute businessman, but this did not show in his romantic relationships. What was wrong with him? He couldn't very well confess to Araceli at this moment because that would defeat the whole purpose of the engagement. However, he needed help formalizing this arrangement because if Lyra spoke to the media about it, he'd be screwed, not to mention a total laughingstock.

As he considered his options, he received a text message from his old college friend Kian Watts, who just happened to be a high-powered attorney in Los Angeles. Even though Kian's specialty was Pacific Rim corporate law, Kian would know precisely what to do. For example, he could prepare a non-disclosure agreement for Lyra to sign and any other relevant documents that would protect him and Lyra from scandal and guard his assets. Someone at his firm would surely have a precedent for those documents. This was Hollywood, after all. They made plans via text to meet in person the following day.

He made a point of tracking down Lyra. He wanted to talk to her and explain why he did what he did. He also wanted to make sure that she wouldn't blow his cover.

"Dr. Brunet, Lyra, I know you think I'm an ass, but could we please speak for a moment?" he asked her gently, without a trace of the pompous tone that had previously come through in his voice.

"Yes, Mr. Rush?" Lyra worked hard to keep her tone rigid. It was difficult. She was excited, and she didn't want to admit it.

"I think we should try and be on a first name basis, and I'm wondering if we could exchange phone numbers?" he asked, almost shyly.

They put each other's contact information into their cell phones, both of them still behaving awkwardly.

"I'd like to take you shopping sometime soon because I'd like to buy you an engagement ring," Dante said nonchalantly. "Maybe we could go to Tiffany on Rodeo Drive? What time do you get off work today? Do you have the time?"

"I'm actually about to wrap up in about an hour. Does that suit you?"

"Yes, thanks. I'll stay with my mother, and perhaps you can find me on your way out?"

"I know you're technically here on vacation. My car is in the employee parkade. Would you like me to drive us? Then I can drop you off at your hotel afterward?"

"Thank you, that would be great."

As soon as she did her rounds, Lyra went to find Dante in Araceli's room.

"There's my brilliant future daughter-in-law," Araceli whispered as enthusiastically as she could. "I'm so proud that my son will marry a beautiful, capable doctor. He told me that you're going ring shopping tonight. You have my blessing."

"Please just rest, Ms. Rush. We'll see you tomorrow," Lyra spoke to her kindly, knowing she was completely in the dark and already anticipating her disappointment when her son finally revealed the truth.

"Goodbye, Maman. I'll see you tomorrow," Dante said as he kissed her gingerly on the forehead.

As they drove together out of the hospital parking lot, Lyra realized that she was completely unprepared for the scenario of fake dating a former television star and model. When she had to stop her vehicle and swipe her keycard, four paparazzi encircled the car, taking nonstop pictures of both of them. It was shocking and unexpected and it made her really nervous. Thank goodness Dante was essentially a C-list celebrity because if he had been an A-lister, she could only imagine what the paparazzi would do to them.

Dante picked up on her disorientation immediately. "Just pause, smile at me, and let them get their shot. Then move on, and they'll back away."

Lyra followed his directions, and they behaved as he had predicted. "Is this every day for you?" she wondered.

"Yes, this is my normal life, and it's about to become your normal life, too," he told her ruefully.

Once safely inside the Tiffany boutique, they browsed through the engagement rings in private. Lyra selected a four-carat Lucida solitaire diamond set in platinum. She wanted a classic, unfussy design that she could wear to work.

"You can keep it after," he told her as she dropped him off at the Beverly Hills Hotel.

Lyra blushed, thinking she would want to keep this fabulous gift from him. He was Dante Rush.

"Do you think I could take you on a proper date tomorrow night? So that we can get to know one another just a little bit? I would really like that."

"Sure, we can do that. I should be done with work tomorrow at around the same time," Lyra not only wanted to be accommodating, but she was also very intrigued. She wondered what going to a restaurant with a celebrity would feel like. Would she be wearing the ring all day? What would people say?

"Thank you, Lyra. I'll see you tomorrow at the hospital. Good night."

"Good night, Dante," she said before she drove away, her engagement ring sitting in a blue box on her passenger seat.

A Mere Formality

GOD HELP HIM. He liked her. Dante didn't know if it was the power of suggestion or what, but Lyra was seriously getting under his skin. He couldn't pinpoint when he became attracted to her or even why because Lyra was not his usual type at all. Dante tended to only date models, and Lyra was relatively petite. Everything about her was small and delicate. As much as he enjoyed having a pair of slender 36-inch-long legs wrapped around his neck, there was something quite intriguing and classically feminine about a woman of a smaller stature than him. Even though Lyra was clearly an accomplished woman, fully capable of taking care of herself, some intangible quality about her made him want to take care of her, to protect her.

Perhaps it was Lyra's intellectual capabilities that had aroused his interest. After all, his usual model girlfriends were barely intelligent enough to read a fashion magazine cover to cover, let alone pore over a medical chart. His standard types were in the picture so that he would have a plus one for events, someone to take luxury vacations and engage in lots of consensual sex with. In Dante's experience, models were typically so undernourished in terms of their food intake that their appetite for sex was rabid. Having dabbled in modeling himself, Dante could attest that the stereotypes of models were pretty much true. Maybe he had enjoyed dating models because their work commitments were so rare that, except for the various fashion weeks, they were always free to travel with him on a schedule that coincided with his own needs.

Lyra had challenged him from the very beginning. Quite the opposite of the way most women related to him, Lyra had not been visibly impressed when they met. Typically, women were all over him because of his good looks, the fame attached to his mother, and the fact that he was a self-made multi-millionaire. Most models made enough money to get by. Still, they knew their careers would have a limited lifespan. They wanted to secure their future by marrying wealthy business-men, actors, or rock stars. This was common knowledge in the industry. For years Dante had been taking advantage of these models who wanted to date him, knowing full well that they were looking for relationships with long-term potential. In contrast, he just wanted to have fun.

Dante was painfully aware that he had misjudged Lyra when they first met. It had been colossally wrong for him to call the higher-ups in the medical world. Asking for a more senior—preferably male—cardiologist to replace her as his mother's principal caregiver. Looking back on his behavior, he wished he could undo it because her first impression of him was negative. Now, he had compounded the problem by insisting that she participate in this sham of an engagement to speed up his mother's recovery. Thank goodness Lyra hadn't been dating anyone. Otherwise, she would have completely rejected him.

Dante smiled, recalling the intense fire in Lyra's eyes as she began to understand what he was doing in Araceli's hospital room. She could have easily blown up and told Araceli that

Dante was a complete fraud, that they hadn't even touched, and that the last thing she would ever do was marry him. Unless he was mistaken, he thought he had detected a spark of excitement, maybe even the potential of some chemistry, between himself and Lyra. Dante had given her his word to keep it all business and set her free as soon as Araceli could withstand the disappointment. If he had physical urges where Lyra was concerned, he would need to snuff them out. He could only imagine how angry she would get if things got physical between them, she got her hopes up, and then he dropped her. He felt that he couldn't bring himself to treat Lyra as cavalierly as he had treated Jaime, for example, simply because Lyra was a higher quality of a person.

When he arrived at Kian's office, his old friend welcomed him with a firm handshake and an accompanying pat on the back. Like him, Kian had aged into his mid-thirties very well. He was tall and solidly built. All through college, Kian had played pro baseball, and between undergrad and law school, he had played for the L.A. Dodgers. He was a fan favorite for five years, and when an injury sidelined him, he went to law school. As soon as he began practicing law, his charisma and name recognition made him a rising star, and clients flocked to him. The fact that he was a native Japanese speaker with wealthy family business roots in the Pacific Rim made him a natural fit for his niche.

"It's been too long since your last trip to California," Kian's tone was genuine. During their college years, the two men had been inseparable. When Kian was playing baseball, Dante had been his wingman, and together they had enjoyed the fruits of the playboy lifestyle. Later, while Dante was acting, Kian was busy going to law school, passing the bar, and building a reputation as one of the leading authorities on Asia-Pacific mergers and acquisitions and international customs and trade law. Recently, the two men had become reacquainted as business partners in a joint venture, a luxury commercial-residential mixed-use complex in Singapore.

Kian had been in a long-term relationship with a woman that ultimately failed because she had refused to sign a prenuptial agreement. Not that Kian was greedy or underhanded, but he explained to Dante that something had seemed off about her during the last few months of their relationship. His firm partners and wider circle of friends all had wives, and most of them had children. Kian had been playing the field for years and was starting to feel like he wanted an actual life partner, a woman to plan his future and start a family with. His girlfriend had been resistant to any discussion related to family planning. When she refused to sign a prenup that was the straw that broke the camel's back.

His desire to settle down went beyond simply wanting a date for black tie events, like the one he had attended a few weeks ago for the Smart Heart Start Society at the Beverly Wilshire Hotel. His law firm had bought a table, and it felt like he was the only man in attendance without a committed woman. If he didn't know better, he would have thought something was wrong with him. While his ego was smaller than Dante's, his intuition told him that there really wasn't anything that mattered on his end, and he just needed to keep an open mind.

"As you know, my mother suffered a massive heart attack less than two weeks ago," Dante explained to his friend.

"The newspapers reported that it was a widowmaker heart attack and that she's lucky to be alive."

"Exactly," he continued. "I'm sure you recall that Araceli has been after me for years to get married and settle down. In a moment of poor judgment and utter desperation for her to regain her zest for life—"

"Oh no. Don't tell me you got married, and now we need to clean up the mess," Kian interrupted.

"Not that bad," Dante went on, "but still a bit of a pickle. See, I just wanted her to have a reason to get well soon and something to look forward to. Her cardiologist was in the room, and she is a beautiful woman. The right age and wasn't wearing a ring, so I told Maman that we had fallen madly in love during her time in the hospital and that we're engaged to be married."

"And you're telling me now that this presumably self-respecting woman, a career woman whom you barely know, has agreed to this? What is she, a star fucker, or what?"

"No, she's the farthest thing from a star fucker. She's completely unimpressed by me. She agreed to go along with my plan because she wanted to absolve herself of liability if my mother died due to the shock and anger she would feel if she found out that I had made the entire story up. Maman is still in a precarious state, and now is not the time to mess with her stress levels. I've agreed to let the truth come out as soon as Lyra agrees that her condition is sufficiently stable to withstand an emotional shock."

"Did you say, Lyra?" Kian was thinking back to the charity ball. "I think I know who that is. She's on the board of the Smart Heart Start Society."

"That would make sense, given that part of the plan is a $250,000.00 donation to that organization," Dante said. "I've already instructed my financial advisor to complete that donation for me."

"She gave a short speech that night. She's really beautiful, Gabe. You're casting totally against type here. Have you considered that having a real relationship with someone like Dr. Lyra Brunet could bring you emotional satisfaction that you haven't experienced before?"

"Yes, I've considered that, but I may be past the point of redemption with her. We'll have to see where this goes. For the moment, I'm asking you to draw up a non-disclosure agreement so that she can't divulge anything to her friends, family, or to the media. I need that iron-clad NDA, plus a prenup that states that we each just keep what we brought into the marriage."

"You think you'll make it through, from engagement to a wedding?"

"That's the plan," Dante knew that he was going deeper than he really meant to, but with a lie like this, it would be hard to go back.

"Okay, no problem," Kian reassured him. "I'll draw up your documents, but you need to do some sleuthing for me, brother. Your missus showed up at the charity ball with the most stunning redhead I have ever seen. I want to meet her ginger friend."

Dante laughed, "Forever the wingman, huh? No problem. Consider it done."

First Date

As she got ready for work that morning, Lyra put on her brand-new engagement ring. She had worn it all around the house the previous night and looked at it on her hand in all different lights, just to see what it felt like. The diamond was flawless, an E color, and it looked bold yet classic in its understated setting. She had always liked the Lucida stone, a special, patented diamond cut exclusive to Tiffany & Co. The idea behind the Lucida was that it had the appearance of a modern square-cut design. Yet, it gave off the fire of a brilliant-cut diamond. Looking straight down at it from above, it almost looked like a diamond within a diamond.

At the risk of feeling silly, Lyra had to admit that she loved wearing an engagement ring. Pretty much every woman dreams about what her engagement ring will look like. While there had been no fairy tale love story, nor a real engagement, to accompany her acquisition of this exquisite diamond ring, she allowed herself to enjoy the experience of wearing the ring all the same. After all, she rationalized that if she had to keep up the charade for a few weeks or even a few months, she might enjoy the experience as much as possible.

She had struggled a bit in deciding what she should wear for her first official non-date with Dante. Afraid they would be tailed by photographers, she took a mirror selfie of her outfit to ensure that it would look as good in a photo as it did in real life. After a few false starts, she finally decided on a pair of navy blue vegan leather leggings, a navy blue silk camisole with black lace trim, and a navy blue blazer with a bit of black and white woven into the bouclé fabric. This was appropriate for the crisp spring weather, practical enough to wear for a day at the hospital, yet chic enough to wear straight out to a week-night dinner after work. She selected a pair of black suede pointy-toe Jimmy Choo pumps with four-inch heels and finished the look with her vintage black Chanel double-flap bag. Her curly, black hair was tied neatly into a low ponytail, and she put on minimal makeup with just a hint of sparkle. Finally, her diamond engagement ring polished off the look just perfectly. Her heart fluttered a little bit as she pictured people noticing her ring and reacting to news of her engagement.

Everyone from the unit clerks to the nursing staff noticed her engagement ring when she arrived. People were all atwitter about it. Every time she passed one of the nursing stations, she was aware that people were excitedly talking about her in hushed tones. She was just waiting for the paparazzi, who were still standing vigil for Araceli outside the hospital entrance, to pick up on the story, and she wasn't entirely sure she was prepared. Theo was the first of her colleagues to ask her about it, point blank.

"What the fuck?"

From anyone else, Theo's initial reaction would have been highly offensive. From her favorite work friend, however, she just laughed, trying to figure out how she would explain this one without having him see right through her. They had been close buddies for so long that she thought he would probably figure it out.

"Why, Dr. Saunders, whatever do you mean?" Lyra asked him in mock surprise, laughing, holding her hand over her heart to fully display her enormous diamond ring.

"Well, it would seem that you were lamenting your lack of a boyfriend just last week, and yet today, you show up wearing a skating rink on your left ring finger. How did that happen?"

Lyra felt terrible lying to her close friend. She vowed that Theo would be the next person to whom she would reveal the truth because, after Michaela, he was the closest thing to her family. She couldn't stand the thought of losing the confidence of someone who mattered to her over Dante, who would, in all likelihood, turn out to be a fair-weather friend. Who knew if they would even be in touch after the truth came out?

"Actually, it turns out that Mr. Right was right there in front of me, and I just needed to open my eyes."

"What? Are you engaged to someone we work with?" Theo's face revealed that he was mentally going through potential candidates in his mind, trying to figure out who Lyra was talking about.

"No, silly, it's Dante Rush, our favorite patient's son," Lyra cautiously revealed.

Theo's mouth dropped open, and he just looked at her, waiting for more. Lyra stayed quiet because she knew what Theo was about to say next.

"But you hate him because he's an asshole. In fact, as I recall, he's the asshole who tried to have you removed from Araceli Rush's acute care team. He's that much of an asshole. So much so, in fact, that you deliberately avoided checking on our patient until you made sure that Dante was not in the room," Theo still wasn't tracking.

Lyra knew that not much got past Theo; he knew her too

well. "Alright, Sherlock, you caught me," she hated lying to him, but still, she let the words come out of her mouth. "I avoided Dante because we had already secretly started seeing one another. I didn't want to raise any eyebrows with the administration, even though I wasn't dating a patient. We just wanted to make it official before coming out with the news."

"Okay," Theo said slowly, and Lyra could see the wheels spinning inside his head because she felt like he still wasn't buying her story. "Okay, well then, please allow me to congratulate you. I'm really happy for you, Lyra. Really happy." He made his voice sound happy, but Lyra could hear the confusion behind his words.

She put a bright smile on her face and reassured him that the engagement was exciting news. "I'll call upon Rowan for her wedding planning tips. Now, I'm going to visit my delightful future mother-in-law."

Lyra was sidelined by a million new cases, and her clinic took longer than usual. It was the end of her day when she finished making all her notes and went to see Araceli.

"And how is my favorite cardiac patient today?" Lyra asked brightly as she walked into Araceli's room. Araceli turned her face towards her and opened her eyes.

"I'm just feeling a little sleepy, my dear," she answered in a dulcet voice. Noticing Lyra's shiny new engagement ring as she was fingering her intravenous bag, she added, "Please let me take a closer look at this ring that my son has given you."

Lyra let Araceli hold her hand to admire the ring.

"I think your son has very sophisticated taste, Ms. Rush."

Even though she found it difficult to speak, her breaths weren't coming as easily as she would have liked. Araceli managed to say, "Araceli, you must please call me Araceli."

Lyra patted her hand to let her know that she would. Dante swept into the room, bringing his mother a fresh bouquet of spring flowers. It didn't take him long to notice his mother's low energy level. He was concerned that she had taken a turn for the worse. Looking at Lyra, Dante didn't have to ask the question; she gave him a reassuring look.

"There you are. I'm so happy to see you," Lyra smiled at her fake fiancé. She was unable to ignore how sexy he looked in his fitted chinos, button-down shirt with the top few buttons undone, and cotton sports jacket. Even his shoes were cool Italian pointy-toed loafers. He was just so sophisticated, and she knew it was all acting for him, but for a brief moment, she didn't care.

"My dear Lyra," Dante's voice was like silk. "I've made reservations for us at the Polo Lounge at the Beverly Hills Hotel. Will that be alright?"

"I love it there," she replied with an easy smile.

"Maman, is it alright with you if I take my beautiful fiancée out to eat? Do you need anything? Are you comfortable?" he inquired.

It took a moment for Araceli to find her voice. With a tired smile, she reassured him that they could go and that she would be fine.

Once again, Lyra drove them to their destination at the Beverly Hills Hotel. Dante was using a car service for himself. Still, since Lyra was leaving work for the day anyway, it was nicer—and more convenient—for them to travel together. As before, paparazzi were photographing them as they exited the hospital parkade, and yet more photographers scouting shots at the Polo Lounge, which was notorious for its celebrity clientele.

"Okay, Mr. Big Shot," Lyra said, only half-jokingly. "You need to sort yourself out and buy a car or get a driver because I just can't handle this. By now, we've figured out you'll stay in Los Angeles longer than just a holiday."

"I understand," Dante laughed. "This isn't fair to you. Trust me, I'm already on it. I have an appointment at the Tesla dealership tomorrow. We can get through tonight, I promise."

As they pulled up to the valet parking stand, they both got out of the vehicle, and Lyra handed the keys to the valet. Although the photographers stayed far enough back to be polite, all the attention still made her nervous. Dante must have sensed this because he placed his hand on the small of her back as he guided her toward the restaurant. He could see that she was shaking a little bit. He wanted to keep her as calm and comfortable as possible, especially since he planned to discuss the NDA and prenup that Kian had drafted for him.

Lyra inhaled the warm night air, fragrance from the blooms in the hotel gardens. It was a welcome change from the sterile hospital, where all she could smell was ammonia and harsh sanitizers. Maybe it was the stimulation from her beautiful environment, or perhaps she was letting herself fall under Dante's spell. Whatever it was, she felt tingly when he placed his hand on her back, with just enough pressure to let her know he was with her, yet not so firm as to be domineering. She really liked how he was touching her at this moment. She mused that she hadn't dated anyone in a while, and even a fake relationship with Dante Rush wasn't a terrible place to start. With a touch of reticence, she could feel herself softening her stance toward this beautiful—yet clueless and egotistical— man. Maybe she would get used to all the attention to the point where she was more comfortable.

As they approached the entrance, they stepped in together. Dante casually slipped his arm around her waist, drawing Lyra's whole body closer toward him. This was a bold move, and Lyra wondered if he always played these emotional games. She was fully aware of their arrangement and had no illusions about an actual future with Dante, but there was something in his demeanor. Lately, that seemed to have shifted. Lyra wondered if seeing his mother—the person who had been the one constant in his life—come so close to death had flipped on his sensitivity switch. There was less of the puffed-up, self-important jackass and more of a lonely man looking to try and make things right in his world. Only time would tell who won out.

The waitress seated them in an intimate booth. Dante didn't hesitate to order the oysters and caviar for them to start, followed by lobster linguine for him and seared branzino for her. He also ordered a bottle of Chablis for them to share, plus sparkling water. Lyra couldn't help but wonder if this kind of extravagance was just a normal dinner for him or if he was trying to impress her.

"Lyra, I know you've had a very long day at work. Thank you for agreeing to this plan of mine, which I understand has upset your world quite significantly," his tone was almost apologetic. His voice was so smooth that Lyra probably would have agreed to anything he might have asked her.

"Well, you did buy me this absolutely spectacular diamond engagement ring," Lyra teased with a smile. She held her ring to admire it, forgetting for a moment that a paparazzo would photograph her in that silly pose.

Dante laughed. "Well, I might as well make it fun for you, right? Seriously, though, our engagement has definitely brought Maman's spirits up. Now that she's thinking about planning our wedding, even from a hospital bed, I can tell she feels relieved that everything will turn out alright for all of us."

"Honestly, Dante, I only agreed to your plan because I, too, had a very close relationship with my mother. She raised me by herself, and we really supported one another. I still think about her every day. Make no mistake, she would be absolutely opposed to your little plan, but I agreed because I know what it's like to lose someone you love."

"Would it be alright if I asked what happened to your mother?" Dante queried in a tone that expressed genuine concern.

"She was diagnosed with stage three lung cancer while I was still a resident, and she fought hard. However, the cancer spread, and she lost her battle a few years ago. Even though you weren't exactly my favorite person, when I recognized the panic on your face and your fear of losing Araceli, I couldn't honestly say no to you."

"I'm sorry you had to go through all that, Lyra. I wish that I could have known your mother too. I doubt I would have been able to charm her." As he said this, a playful glint was in his eye to lighten the mood.

"Thank you," she said. "Now, where do we go from here?"

"Araceli would like us to arrange an engagement party," he began. "Even though she'll still be in the hospital, we could arrange to live stream the party so that she can watch it from her hospital bed. I have a large bungalow at this hotel, and it would be very simple to cater the party here. How would you feel about that?"

"When did you think we should have this party? Who would we invite? Do you even have any friends or family here?"

"Only a few," Dante replied unenthusiastically. "This engagement party would be more for Araceli so that her circle of friends hears our news. I have one close friend here, Kian Watts, but everyone else is window dressing."

"Well, my best friend Michaela Moses, who will be my maid of honor, would be invited, as well as a few of my colleagues from the hospital, whom I consider good friends. I don't have any family here."

"I suppose that our guest list will be short." Lyra thought she detected some relief in Dante's voice, as if he didn't want to overdo the fake engagement. "My friend Kian will probably get along really well with Michaela. When I told him about you, he remembered hearing you gave a speech at a charity ball a few weeks ago, and he mentioned that your titian-haired friend was quite a beauty."

"I'm sure that Michaela will look forward to that," Lyra giggled within herself. This whole fake dating, a former television star game, was fun. Still, she was afraid she might be getting herself into dangerous territory. She didn't want to fall for Dante and all his charms only to have him suddenly disappear from her life entirely. That would hurt.

Having enjoyed a luxurious dinner, Dante raised the issue of the non-disclosure agreement and the prenup. Of course, Lyra had to agree.

"Yes, of course, I have no problem with it," she assured him. "I'll meet with my lawyer, review the documents, sign them, and return them to you. Please don't worry about that."

As Dante walked Lyra back to the valet desk to retrieve her car after dinner, he kept one arm wrapped around her slim waist. She enjoyed the physical intimacy, and the closeness that she felt with him, even though there wasn't any emotional intimacy. Perhaps that will change, she thought to herself, or perhaps not. I'll have to be okay with it either way.

Before she left, with paparazzi waiting to snap their pictures, Dante put one fingertip on Lyra's chin, gently turning her face towards his, and kissed her lightly. It was the kind of kiss designed to present the right angles to the camera, like a television kiss. It was gentle and sweet and took Lyra's breath away just a little bit. Without saying another word, Lyra got into her car. She drove away, and Dante walked home to his bungalow at the hotel.

Engagement Party

LYRA WAS apprehensive about throwing an engagement party, but Araceli was insistent. Dante assured her that the event would lend legitimacy to their little make-believe love story and maybe even help to speed up his mother's recovery. The problem was that Lyra could feel herself starting to enjoy Dante's company more than she cared to admit. The last thing she wanted to do was accidentally develop real feelings for a knave who would abandon her as soon as his mother's prognosis for recovery was stable.

Since their first date, she and Dante spent quite a bit of time together over the past few days, both inside and outside the hospital. As much as she wished it wasn't true, she could tell that Dante was just a lonely, kind soul. More than anything, she could see that he was nothing more than a devoted son who was desperately searching for a way to bring his mother back to her usual vibrant self. Having lost her mother, she could imagine how strong their bond was. She wanted his inner child to satisfy Araceli with this engagement party. When Lyra allowed her imagination to run a bit wild, she fantasized that Dante would actually fall head over heels in love with her and that he would whisk her away to his castle in France. She would never have to work another all-night on-call shift again.

Luckily for her, Dante and his mother had the means and influence to plan a glamorous party quickly. Lyra's guest list was relatively small, and Dante and his mother's guests totaled about twenty-five people. This meant that there would be a lot of Hollywood types at their party, people who might be looking at Lyra and judging her. She was slightly nervous because this event was out of her comfort zone.

Thankfully, Michaela had taken her shopping. They had selected a beautiful Valentino cocktail dress with cap sleeves and a hemline higher than usual for Lyra, who normally dressed conservatively for work. The dress was covered in oversized gold sequins that created a beautiful array of dappling light whenever she moved. The soft golden tone of her dress contrasted beautifully with the rich mocha tones of her skin. Her Stuart Weitzman Nudist sandals, with four-inch stiletto heels, completed the look, and the height gave her extra confidence. Dante generously gave her a credit card and sent her shopping. She had to admit that she enjoyed the perks of her made-up engagement. Still, there was a fine line between having fun and taking advantage of him, and she didn't want to cross that line—this wasn't a Pretty Woman situation!

Lyra had carefully packed an overnight bag to bring to Bungalow Five at the Beverly Hills Hotel. After discussing it with Dante, they decided that she should spend the night with him after the party. He showed her to her own bedroom, complete with an ensuite, so she would feel secure in the knowledge that if she wanted privacy, she would have it. She appreciated this gesture, but at the same time, she was worried about herself. This engagement party was really taking their situation out into the public domain, and she wondered how she would handle the fallout when everything inevitably comes to a halt.

Even though they barely kissed, Lyra had gotten enough of a taste of Dante to know they would have good chemistry together. His kiss tasted good to her, and his lips were just the right pillowy soft texture, yet were manly at the same time. His experience as an actor must have enabled him to kiss someone so deftly when no emotion was attached. She wasn't entirely sure why she had made this choice, but Lyra had packed a brand new, unopened box of condoms in her overnight bag. She didn't know if she was hopeful, optimistic, or overly cautious. Still, she would have condoms on hand if she needed them. Since Dante had told her that his bungalow had its own private swimming pool, she had also packed her new gold bikini, with the cheekier than usual bottoms and the uplifting underwire bra, complete with a gauzy gold shirt-style cover-up.

Araceli had hired an event planner. A wonderfully fussy gay man named Nathan, dressed in a slim-cut, muted coral pantsuit, was directing the catering staff and the florist. Even if it wasn't a true blue romance, Lyra couldn't stop herself from getting swept up in the excitement that was to be her engagement party. She felt like she was the star of her own Hallmark Original Movie. Complete with the false starts, the supportive friends, the uncertainty, the betrayal, and finally, the happy ending. Then she shook her head as if that would bring her back to reality. She had to remind herself that all of this was temporary and that within a few weeks, as soon as Araceli was stable enough so that hearing the truth wouldn't shock her heart, the bubble would burst. She would return to her normal life.

Nathan had ordered a beautiful selection of hors d'oeuvres, and the Veuve Clicquot champagne would flow freely all night, in addition to a tended cocktail bar. Vases of hibiscus flowers were nestled in every corner to brighten the space. Araceli and Dante had briefed Lyra on all their expected guests, but she was still nervous. This whole Hollywood world of theirs was a far cry from how Lyra had grown up. Even though she lived and practiced medicine in Los Angeles, she didn't have any friends in the industry. She didn't want to appear insecure in front of Dante because she wanted to hold up her end of the bargain, and she also wanted him to like her genuinely.

Once he was ready for the party, Dante came out to be with Lyra and to just go over details while they waited for their guests to arrive. He was wearing a pale blue-gray slim-cut suit with a white dress shirt. The top two buttons were undone to reveal just a glimpse of his smooth, toned chest. A blue and white patterned silk pocket square was expertly arranged in his jacket pocket. He wore a slim tan suede belt that perfectly matched his elegant loafers. To Lyra, he looked like he had just stepped off a yacht. When he came close to greet her, she could smell his cologne. She involuntarily nestled into the crook of his neck before realizing that perhaps she should try and maintain a little distance. However, Dante gave her a look that told her he didn't seem to mind, then took her hand, and let his lips brush hers in a quick, casual kiss.

"I hope you don't mind, Lyra, but Kian has asked me to introduce him to your friend Michaela at the party tonight," Dante began, just a little bit shyly.

"Your lawyer friend? The one who used to play baseball?"

"That's the one," he continued. "When I met with him to discuss our arrangement, he asked me if you were the same Lyra Brunet who had made a speech at the charity ball."

"He was there?" Lyra asked, surprised. "We thought everyone there was married. I think that was before I met you."

"Yes, well, Kian is not married. He never has been. He also

76

told me that he was very impressed by your speech. He wanted to be introduced to the beautiful strawberry blonde who appeared to be your plus one that night. He doesn't know why he didn't just walk up and introduce himself to the both of you. As you know, men don't always make the best decisions."

Lyra laughed despite herself. "Oh, I think Michaela would really like to meet him. She won't be shy, and I think she's on her way here now."

"That's fantastic," Dante beamed, and they shared a conspiratorial smile as people started arriving. While Nathan took care of the party details, Dante took center stage as a suave host and introduced Lyra to all of Araceli's friends, a few family members, and some of Dante's business partners. Nathan had arranged to live stream the party so Araceli could participate remotely. Lyra had grown to really like Araceli. She was a good patient, very kind, always in a good mood person, and nice to all the staff. She felt a bit of a twinge at the thought of disappointing her very soon.

"Kian is super, amazingly hot, and intelligent," out of nowhere, Michaela came right up behind her, offering Lyra a second glass of champagne. "I can't believe he didn't just come to talk to me at the gala that night. Thank goodness for your fake engagement; otherwise, I would never have met Kian. No judgment if I let him take me home tonight."

"Of course, I know, I met him earlier, and he's terrific. You have my blessing," Lyra replied with a wink, admiring her friend's beautiful peaches and cream complexion, with its sprinkling of light freckles across her delicate nose and high cheekbones. Michaela seemed to have a glint of mischief in her emerald green eyes, and Lyra could see that her cheeks were flushed with excitement. "By the way, I love what you're wearing!" Tonight, Michaela had chosen an ice blue silk satin knee-length dress with ivory lace trim, chiffon cap sleeves, and an open back. The dress seemed to move with her in a dreamy, fluid motion whenever she moved. Lyra could understand why Kian Watts would be captivated by her friend.

Suddenly, the hairs on the back of Lyra's neck stood up, and she was overcome by an inexplicable feeling of unease. She looked for Dante and noticed that he appeared to be in conversation with a very attractive blonde woman. Lyra didn't recognize her as one of the people whom Araceli and Dante had described to her to expect as a party guest. Still, at the same time, the woman looked familiar.

As Lyra approached them, she saw that Dante didn't look all comfortable. "Lyra," he practically choked, "this is Jaime. She and I used to be in a relationship. It's over now, as you can see, and Jaime is here as someone's guest."

Jaime held out her hand, and Lyra shook it reluctantly. "I was shooting a campaign for a local beauty brand, and I took this opportunity to come and congratulate Dante." There was neither any sincerity, nor warmth at all, in Jaime's voice. She looked Lyra up and down with disdain, then turned to Dante to say, "Keep in mind what I said," before walking away.

"What was that about?" Lyra asked him.

"Okay, Jaime and I were in a relationship, which ended just before I came to meet Maman in Los Angeles. She clearly didn't support our relationship and was just looking for an excuse to see me. I'm sorry, Lyra, she treated you disrespectfully, and I'm hoping she's on her way out."

"It's fine, I know you have a past, but I didn't expect anyone like her to show up at our engagement party."

"Please don't let Jaime get under your skin. She's a nobody, and as far as I'm concerned, you're the smartest and most beautiful woman here. I hope that we don't let her spoil our evening." As Dante spoke to her, Lyra thought she could hear a tenderness in his voice.

Wanting to stay positive and focus on enjoying her party, Lyra kept circulating, eventually landing with Michaela and

Kian. As the three of them chatted, she could tell there was serious chemistry between her best friend and Kian. It's too bad our relationship is a hoax, she thought, because it would have been fun to double date and take long weekends together. Then, out of the corner of her eye, Lyra could see that Jaime had circled back to Dante now that Lyra had left his side. Jaime must have thought she was safely out of earshot because she uttered just about the vilest thing a person could say at a celebratory event.

"Let me guess, Dante...you got her pregnant."

Lyra's face fell when she heard these harsh words. She involuntarily let go of her glass of champagne, which fell silently to the plush carpet and spilled rather unceremoniously at her feet. Nathan witnessed the entire event and came over wordlessly to tidy up the mess. Jaime looked straight into Lyra's eyes, not even trying to conceal the sneer on her lips.

"You need to leave, Dante said to Jaime under his breath. "Now," and he walked over to Lyra, gently slipping his arm around her waist.

Lyra was relieved when she turned around and came face to face with Theo and Rowan. They had arrived a bit late after both had finished their shifts at the hospital. Theo gave her a broad smile because, as her steadfast friend, he had deliberately chosen to be happy for her. Rowan took Lyra up in her warm embrace, in such a close and joyful hug that Lyra could smell her signature sweet scent, Givenchy's Dahlia Divin. Her soft yellow tulle babydoll dress perfectly matched her sunny disposition.

"Ooooh! I had no idea all of this was happening," Rowan gushed. "When Theo told me, I just about died! I've been so wrapped up in planning my own wedding that I've totally had blinders on when it comes to what's happening in everyone else's life. Let me see the ring!"

Lyra dutifully displayed her ring finger, and Rowan's jaw

dropped in mock excitement as she pretended she had to cover her eyes. "The glare! I'm blinded by the fire reflecting off of that enormous stone!"

They laughed, and Lyra replied, "I know, Rowan, it's been a whirlwind. I'm so happy that you and Theo could make it. I could probably use some advice for planning the wedding."

"Okay, except that something tells me your budget will be way bigger than ours."

Lyra rolled her eyes and nodded in agreement with her friend. "Probably. I think Araceli will want to take care of most of the details for us. I love what you're wearing. You look so good in yellow." Thank goodness for Theo and Rowan's distraction because it enabled Lyra to shake away the negative thoughts that Jaime's rude comments had brought into her head. She had enough insecurities to deal with.

The rest of the party was smooth, pleasant, and uneventful. Except for Jaime, every guest genuinely congratulated Lyra and Dante. Even though she knew what was going on between them would end soon, Lyra enjoyed meeting and getting to know the important people in Araceli and Dante's lives. For his part, Dante appeared to have made an effort to engage with the people on Lyra's guest list.

After all, the guests had gone home, and the staff had tidied up the bungalow. Dante and Lyra said goodnight to one another, just a little bit awkwardly. He put his hands gently on her shoulders and stroked her arms down to her elbows. She felt a frisson of delight at his touch. She couldn't help it— Dante was such a beautiful man, and for the moment, he was all hers.

"I really want to kiss you," he said huskily, his eyes looking into hers, his lips so close that she could feel his breath as he exhaled the words. Silently, she nodded, and he took her face in his hands to kiss her thoroughly, deeply, and decisively. As their kiss deepened, Lyra felt herself relax, and she put her arms around him. He moved one hand to the nape of her neck, his fingers lightly stroking her hair. Their lips seemed to fit perfectly together, as did their bodies. Finally, before he took the kiss to the next level, Dante pulled back from their embrace.

"I should probably let you go to sleep, Lyra. I'll see you tomorrow morning at breakfast. Maybe we can order room service and eat outside by the pool." There was a glint of seduction in his eyes, which Lyra knew she would have difficulty resisting if he persisted.

Lyra nodded, still hypnotized by their kiss and unable to form the words to reply. She retreated to her bedroom, and Dante walked across the living room, and then disappeared into his own bedroom for the night.

The Friend Zone

AFTER THEIR ENGAGEMENT PARTY, Lyra spent the weekend with Dante at Bungalow Five at the Beverly Hills Hotel. She was treated like a princess and couldn't help but enjoy herself. Dante was actually a lot of fun to be around. Obviously, but they never would have met for having been thrown together by their present circumstances. However, as they were currently an item, albeit fictional, Lyra had decided to enjoy the entire experience.

She and Dante had become friends by enjoying some leisure time together. After breakfast each morning, she enjoyed listening to him make his business calls, then they would go for a swim. She would go to work, and he joined her in the afternoons to visit Araceli at the hospital and meet with Nathan about their wedding plans. They had enjoyed a few intimate dinners together and a double-date dinner with Michaela and Kian. Dante's kisses were consistent but not progressing. Similarly, Araceli's health was steady but not progressing to the level where Lyra could confidently discharge her.

Lyra chalked up Dante's holding pattern to holding up his

part of the bargain and not taking things to extremes. That said, she begun fantasizing about what it would feel like to be with him. She could feel his nicely muscled arms, chest, and shoulders whenever he embraced her. Her mind kept wondering at areas she really shouldn't be, given the finite nature of their non-relationship. Seeing him in his swimsuit and robe at the hotel only encouraged her sexual fantasies. Lyra knew what was going on, but it still puzzled her that he wasn't even trying to seduce her. Maybe the progression of their emotional relationship was just a figment of her imagination.

She took two weeks off of work to attend Theo and Rowan's wedding and then focused on her faux wedding planning, followed by a week of downtime after her nuptials. Araceli had been insistent about her and Dante scheduling their nuptials for the following week, which meant that Lyra needed to use up an extra two weeks of her saved vacation. She didn't see the harm in taking extra time off since all of her patients, including Araceli, were being well taken care of by the other doctors on staff. Besides, it would seem unnatural to schedule her wedding, then after that, go back to work the next day. She and Dante were doing their best to make everything seem like a natural progression, albeit completely rushed.

"So, for your friends' wedding, Theo and Rowan, do you think we should take notes?" Dante was half teasing, but Lyra could sense that he was starting to get nervous about their own wedding, which was now just days away.

"Are you starting to get worried? I'm fine if you want to tell Araceli we made the decision in haste. I'm sure she'll be able to handle the news."

"Not at all," he shrugged. "She adores you and will not be pleased if we cancel our wedding. I meant that maybe we should copy some of the schmaltzy things they do to look more natural and down-to-earth when we tie the knot."

"But Dante," Lyra felt comfortable enough to tease him a little bit. "You're not down-to-earth at all. You're the son of a major movie star, a living legend, and I'm the first non-famous woman you've ever been linked to. Why would you try and pretend to be something you're not? I think the pretense of our marriage is more than enough, wouldn't you say?"

"Touché, my dear Lyra." Then after a pause, he ventured, "It just seems to me that by now, we would have moved in together, don't you think? I love taking up residence at the Beverly Hills Hotel, but maybe we could live together part-time at your home? Maman's been asking me what your house is like, and I keep telling her that you still haven't brought me home."

Lyra sighed and pretended to roll her eyes at his suggestion. "Is this your subtle way of asking me to make up a guest room for you?"

"Maybe," he grinned.

"You know I live in a normal house, not a castle or Beverly Hills. My home is nothing like what you're accustomed to."

"Lyra, yes, and you're nothing like what I'm accustomed to, either. You've challenged me in ways that I hadn't anticipated."

"Okay, Dante, then today, let's go to my house to get ready for the Saunders' wedding, and you can have a taste of what it's like to be regular. You know I have no staff at home, so we're clear."

He laughed and just shook his head.

There was something so effortlessly seductive about Dante. Maybe it was his boyish charm, or maybe it was the confident way he held her hand, or how he put his arm around her when they walked. Lyra couldn't put her finger on it. Still, all she knew was that he had that je ne sais quoi, that intangible quality that made him irresistible. She had already prepared the guest room next to hers upstairs for Dante to use. She didn't want to admit that she secretly wanted him to sleep with her in her room. Her inner romantic kept thinking that maybe they could flip the script. Dante would see that Lyra was actually the kind of woman he'd been waiting for all his life. She wondered if they had met under different circumstances, whether he would have still found her attractive or if her lack of fame made her too plain for his taste.

"You know, I love your house, Lyra," Dante told her. "It's just right for you at this stage of your life. The Mediterranean style is classic and almost reminds me of home."

"Thank you," she responded. "I hope this room is alright. The décor is neutral, but since it's only temporary, I figured giving you a room with a simple color palette would suffice."

"Of course," he smiled. "Lyra, this is all going to work out just fine. I promise. I'm not going to embarrass you, and I won't do anything to make you wish you hadn't gotten involved. I wouldn't do that to you."

"I know," she whispered, wondering if he ever thought about sleeping with her the same way that she fantasized about him. Dante answered her question by sweeping her into a strong embrace. He kissed her in the upstairs hallway, pressing her back gently against the wall between her master bedroom and his guest room. She relaxed into his kiss and could feel his arousal as he pressed against her. There was no more mystery in that regard. Lyra allowed herself be carried away by his deep kiss. She enjoyed the feeling of his warm, wet lips pressing against hers. His tongue was in her mouth in such a way as to make her want to feel everything.

Lyra was suddenly very aware of where this episode might

be leading. While she wasn't opposed to making love to Dante, they did have an event to get to. It took all her willpower to pull away from him and to remind him that they needed to get ready for Theo and Rowan's wedding on the beach. Dante was breathing hard, too, at this point. He resignedly pulled away, pretending to punch the wall behind her in frustration.

"Then let me just get dressed in my room, and we'll be ready to leave together shortly." Before he let her go, he let his fingers linger just a little longer, entwined with hers. His lips grazed the crook of her neck, traveling up from her collarbone and all the way up to finish with a little nip at her earlobe. Lyra smiled with pleasure at this feeling of long-awaited intimacy. Finally, they let go of one another and went into their rooms to change.

When Lyra emerged from her room, dressed to attend her friends' wedding, Dante was waiting downstairs in the foyer. As he watched her float down the curved staircase, her shoulder-length wavy black hair cascading over her smooth, bare shoulders, he felt himself take a sharp inhale. She was a stunningly beautiful woman—how could he not have noticed how arrestingly pretty she was? This evening, she was wearing a cream chiffon strapless dress fitted through the bodice, whose light layers of ruffles fluttered delicately above her pretty knees. Lyra could tell that Dante liked what he saw, and she smiled at him somewhat coyly.

"My, don't you look handsome tonight," she said, admiring his dark beige, slim-cut linen suit.

"Lyra, thanks, and I have to just tell you that you look so lovely tonight—not wholesome, not angelic, just a classic beauty. And judging by our color scheme, I'd say we're pretty much in sync."

"We do look good together," Lyra agreed. She was still at that uncertain stage with him, where she wasn't confident or comfortable enough to just walk up to him and kiss him. Lyra wanted Dante to be the one to set the pace in that regard. He held out his hand, and she placed her hand in his. He had gone back to being a gentleman, and for the moment, she didn't sense the animal heat she had felt an hour earlier in the upstairs hallway.

"The car service is waiting outside. I'm looking forward to being your plus one tonight, Lyra."

"Me too, Dante, me too."

It was the perfect evening for a small beachside wedding. As Lyra watched two of her good friends get married, she felt wistful. Wishing she would one day find her perfect match, her soul mate, someone who understood her better than anyone else. Over the past few years, Rowan has supported Theo. She had understood how tired he had been during his residency and how stressful it was to write his medical board exams. Their shared history at work and school had brought them incredibly close. Why hadn't Lyra been able to find a similar kind of relationship? She was really happy for her friends. Yet, at the same time, she couldn't understand what was wrong with her that her first wedding would be a fictional fairy tale instead of a love story grounded in reality.

As they sat together observing the ceremony, Lyra could feel Dante's hand stroking hers. She couldn't tell if the gesture was romantic or more on the side of friendship. Whatever it was, she could sense the respect in his touch, and she knew that, at the very least, she had found a new friend in him, and most likely in Araceli too. She wondered how everything would play out at the end of the day once Araceli was out of the hospital. Now that she knew him a little bit better, she could tell that Dante was a decent human being: He was funny, sensitive, and sincere, and the man she knew now barely resembled the puffed-up egomaniac she had met six weeks prior at the hospital. This Dante—her Dante—was genteel.

Michaela had brought Kian as her wedding date, and it was clear that the two of them had serious chemistry. They even looked good together. Kian's tall, muscular physique was a nice counterpart to Michaela's nicely toned petite frame, which had just enough curves to still look soft and feminine. Lyra noticed Kian looking admiringly at her friend while the four of them were having a conversation. She wondered whether people ever caught Dante looking at her in that exact way. It was as if Dante were a painting in a museum, and she had to stand behind the velvet rope to admire him, but she just couldn't find her way into the painting. There was no way for her to access his thoughts and feelings. The businessman in him must have mastered the poker face because he constantly kept her guessing.

After they had danced together for a few songs, Lyra and Dante stood on the sidelines, sipping champagne. He placed one hand gently on the small of her back and kept it there, and Lyra chose to interpret this as a proprietary gesture. Yes, they had their signed contract in place. However, the hopeless romantic inside of Lyra still wanted Dante to wake up and realize that he had actually fallen in love with her. There was no need to set up this elaborate scheme. At first, Lyra didn't want to admit to these feelings. Feelings she feared were childish and contrary to her philosophy of being a self-sufficient, independent woman of substance. However, even the most self-assured career women were allowed to be human and to want the man to fall head over heels in love. It was biological, she rationalized, and it didn't make her any less of a cardiologist or any less of a modern woman.

"You know," Dante began, "when this is all over, I'm going to let you break things off with me, and we'll make that very clear to the press and everyone. I want to make sure that you come out of our short marriage smelling like a rose."

And just like that, Lyra's bubble burst.

"That's very thoughtful of you. I...um...I really...I mean —" she stammered because her mind had been expecting him to say something entirely different, and it would take her a minute to regain her bearings.

"Because the thing is, Lyra," he went on, "I haven't ever dated anyone like you. I've dated women who were smart and beautiful, but you possess this je ne sais quoi. You're a higher quality human being than any girl I've ever met. My mother agrees with me wholeheartedly."

Lyra nodded silently, unsure of what she should say if anything. If she was that amazing, why was Dante still planning to break things off when Araceli was out of the hospital? She must have been mistaken when she thought they were making inroads with physical and emotional intimacy. He must still be an excellent actor, she thought. Damn, how is it possible for me to be so intelligent at work and such a dismal failure when it comes to my romantic life?

"I've been thinking a lot about this. I know that you have a very successful career. Still, I recognize that I've disrupted your life greatly. I hope you don't mind, but I've asked Kian to draw up the legal paperwork to let me pay off the mortgage on your house and all your remaining student loans. I know that you don't specifically need the money, but this is really the only way that I know how to thank you for stepping into this short-term role. It's also my way of making up for being less than polite when I first met you."

"Wow," Lyra breathed. "I wouldn't want to look a gift

horse in the mouth. How can I say no to that? I appreciate the gesture, Dante, but you know I don't need or expect that from you. At first, I was supremely annoyed with you, and I felt really put out. Still, now that I've eased nicely into the role of your fiancée, I'm actually really enjoying myself."

"Then we'll just call it a gesture of friendship, shall we?" he asked, clinking their champagne flutes in a conspiratorial toast.

"To friendship," Lyra agreed quietly and took another sip of her champagne.

Wedding Day

LYRA WOKE up on the day of her own wedding to find the sunshine streaming through her bedroom windows. God help her. She felt joyful. Lyra didn't care if her wedding was real or make-believe because she had sensed a shift in Dante. She could tell that he felt a strong desire to take care of her, and she knew that once their relationship turned physical, he would be all in.

As she rose from her bed, she noticed a trail of white rose petals across the floor, leading her to a handwritten note on her dressing table. It read: "My Dear Lyra, I've returned to the hotel, wanting to keep today traditional. I'll see you at the altar. Yours, Dante."

She went downstairs to make coffee, knowing that Michaela would arrive anytime with pastries. Dante had agreed that it would be best to keep the wedding party small, with Kian as his best man and Michaela as Lyra's maid of honor. Araceli had narrowed down her guest list, so the total number of attendees would be under a hundred. Nathan had taken care of all the details, and since it wasn't the real deal,

Lyra had relinquished control. Araceli had insisted on footing the entire bill, which made Lyra a bit apprehensive. Still, Dante didn't express any concern, so she didn't dwell on it. After all, this event was Dante's idea, and Lyra hadn't done anything wrong or deceptive. If Araceli got mad after the truth came out, that would be Dante's problem. Yes, Lyra felt terrible because she had grown to care about Araceli. Still, she was really just going along with Dante's initiative.

The doorbell rang, and Lyra went to the door to greet her best friend, the only member of her inner circle who knew the real truth. As she opened the door, she burst out laughing. Michaela was holding so many boxes of fancy pastries, lingerie, and makeup kits that her face was completely obscured. All Lyra could see was a mop of red curls sticking out on top.

"Good morning to the world's most beautiful bride," she called out in a singsong voice. "And how are we feeling today? Are you ready to turn on the bridezilla? Is it going to be all about, 'My day, my way'?"

"Ha-ha, very funny," she replied. "Today, Michaela will be a day of magic. I mean, obviously, we both know it's not really real. Still, Dante is a total catch, and what if we were to look at this as an arranged marriage, only different? I mean, obviously, I understand what it is—"

"But you've grown to really like him," Michaela interrupted her friend. "I know, Lyra. You don't have to explain. Kian and I talked about it this morning after we made love... have I mentioned that he's amazing?" They both giggled. "Anyway," she continued, "It's plain to see that Dante has become a changed man after nearly losing Araceli. Kian told me he hasn't mentioned the NDA or the prenup lately, and all he does is wax poetic about you. Those documents Kian drew up might be in the paper shredder after tonight."

"I know, Michaela, and I think I'm getting that vibe from

him. Things are really different now than they were before. I can sense that he's kind of protective of me, and he's definitely turned on when we're together, but he hasn't gone past second base. At this point, I don't know what he's waiting for. Maybe he doesn't want me to get too attached. Who knows? Anyway, today is my wedding day. I'm going to marry a very handsome, super successful actor-turned-model-turned-businessman. Whatever the outcome, this will have been an adventure."

"Kian and I have discussed it—intimately. Dante has fallen for you, and it's only a matter of hours now before your honeymoon officially starts, right?"

"Yes, except that I told him I didn't want to go on a honeymoon. That would be taking the pretense too far, don't you think? Anyway, he said that he understood my position."

Michaela shook her head. "I thought you said that you felt like you were getting married for real, albeit with a very nontraditional start. If you have feelings for him, why wouldn't you spend a honeymoon with him, even just a few nights in Laguna?"

Lyra shook her head. "We're not going to have this conversation right now. If I'm not mistaken, my maid of honor and I are getting ready to experience a day of pure magic. Am I right?" The mood switched from uncertainty and self-doubt to an atmosphere of sheer delight. Together, they drank their coffee and ate pastries, giggling and exchanging sex tips.

The two friends were ready to be pampered when the hair and makeup artists arrived. Both girls wanted to look natural in person yet flawless in pictures. For Michaela, the stylist took advantage of her natural strawberry blonde waves and made them look more polished. Her makeup was a clean wash of peachy blush, shimmering eyeshadow, a touch of liner, mascara, and a coral nude lipstick. This look perfectly complemented the simplicity of her silky satin coral slip dress. As a bridesmaid gift, Lyra had given her friend a gold necklace with a simple gold and diamond crescent moon charm to symbolize the growth and transformation of their friendship and moving into a new phase of life.

Lyra's look was equally simple, just a touch more elegant. The stylist tied her hair half-back and added a few camellia flowers to imbue her with a whimsy. All she needed was some tinted moisturizer for her face to even out her skin tone; a wash of subtle blush, some highlighter on her cheekbones, a dab of pearlescent eyeshadow, some mascara, and a nude lip gloss. Instead of a poofy wedding gown, Michaela had helped her to choose a classic maxi slip dress, made of matte silk crepe in the most delicate of off-white tones, with a simple round neck and an open back that finished in a vee point, just low enough, with a nude lace border along each side going down the edge of the low-cut back. They both wore the same four-inch barely-there patent leather nude stiletto sandals.

The ceremony was held at the Beverly Hills Hotel, where Lyra and Dante would spend the night in Bungalow Five, which he still hadn't checked out of. Nathan had arranged for Araceli to attend their wedding via live stream. All the details had been arranged, including the four-piece band. The garden was candle-lit for their special evening wedding. When she arrived and looked around, all Lyra could think was how lovely everything seemed. How serenely beautiful and how much her mother would have enjoyed getting to know Araceli and Dante.

Upon arrival, the women went straight to the room Kian and Michaela had booked for the night just to freshen up one last time before the ceremony. Nathan came to get them when it was time. As they approached the garden where all the chairs had been set up, it struck Lyra that this was really happening: Dante's plan had come to fruition, and there could be no turning back. She took in a deep breath, and then walked down the aisle behind her maid of honor. Dante and Kian were standing at the altar, flanking the justice of the peace. Dante's eyes met hers, he nodded as if to give her courage, and she held his gaze the entire time as she walked down the aisle.

The ceremony went off without a hitch. Lyra didn't let herself be spooked by the paparazzi who leaped out from behind columns and plants to snap their photos. Instead of a sit-down dinner, they had arranged a generous buffet of hors d'oeuvres, including an oyster bar on ice to add to the glamor. The cocktail bar served everything their guests wanted, and they all danced until after midnight. Lyra enjoyed every single moment of their wedding. Unless Dante had returned to acting, she was confident that he viewed the evening as successful too.

After they had said goodnight to their last guests and Nathan had taken all their gifts back to Lyra's house, she and Dante retired to Bungalow Five, where they enjoyed their first kiss. In the living room, he embraced her with a fervor that she hadn't been expecting. She relished this new sexually daring side of him, thinking that tonight they would finally come together as an actual, real couple.

"Mmmm, Lyra, I've been picturing what's under this dress all evening. I'm so hot that I can barely think straight," he said huskily. His hands traveled up and down her body, over the silk and sliding inside her dress in the back, right down to the very lowest point of the vee.

"I would say it's about time, Dante," she whispered, kissing him back, letting him know how much she enjoyed the feel of his hands on her bare skin.

Just then, Dante's phone rang, totally interrupting their moment. It was Araceli, FaceTiming them, and Lyra couldn't bring herself to be annoyed.

"I just want to congratulate my beautiful son, the love of

my life, my purpose, and my beautiful new daughter-in-law. Seeing you come together in marriage has brought me back to life. I couldn't be happier. Just so you know, I've booked you the honeymoon suite at the Ritz-Carlton Hotel at Dana Point. You can go there tomorrow and enjoy the rest of the week in honeymoon solitude. I won't even call you. That will be your time," Araceli winked conspiratorially.

"Wow, that is so generous. Thank you so much, Araceli. We are so lucky," Lyra did feel fortunate, and she sensed that Araceli's manner with her was very maternal.

"Maman, thank you, and goodnight," Dante ended the call.

Unfortunately, it seemed as though the romantic spell had been broken. Dante's demeanor changed, and he stood there as if he needed to block his next move.

"I've attended a conference at the Ritz-Carlton, Dante, and it's really nice. The setting near the cliffs is spectacular. Araceli is being very generous with us—so much so that I almost can't bear to keep up this charade with her any longer."

Just then, Lyra noticed the change in Dante's face, and she knew she had said the wrong thing. She opened her mouth to backtrack and reframe her statement, but Dante spoke first.

"Well, I thought we might rewrite our script since these past few weeks have been quite special between us. I thought we had perhaps shifted. I was going to ask you to move with me to France, so we could continue an actual relationship together."

"Dante, I have a whole life here, a career, and obligations. I can't just follow you to your castle in France on a lark, especially as a man who plans to annul our marriage as soon as his mother can handle the shock."

This wasn't going as either one of them had planned. They had both started the day with the most romantic of intentions, and it suddenly turned to dust. Dante took her up into a gentle embrace, bent down to kiss her forehead, wished her goodnight, and they each retired to their separate rooms. Each of them was too proud and perhaps feeling too vulnerable to let the other know how they truly felt.

Making Love

Not wanting to disappoint Araceli, they stopped at Lyra's house the following day to pack their bags, then drove together to the resort at Dana Point. After all, it was a very generous and thoughtful wedding gift to send them off to enjoy a few days of seaside luxury and romance. Araceli had the very best intentions where Dante and Lyra were concerned, and it would have been rude to refuse. Besides, since no flight was involved, it hardly qualified as a showy, lavish, over-the-top fake honeymoon. For her part, Lyra knew that her feelings toward Dante had morphed into something that she thought could be love. She felt as though her feelings were reciprocated. Still, she knew that if he was going to come clean, she had to reassure him that she felt the same way and that they could take their leap of faith together.

During the two-hour drive from Beverly Hills to the Ritz-Carlton resort at Dana Point, Dante let one hand rest on Lyra's bare knee. She liked this connection and the sexual tension that went along with it. She couldn't believe they still hadn't slept together, not even on their wedding night. She wondered what he was afraid of—true intimacy, perhaps? Lyra was anything but a pushover, but she couldn't recall having been in any kind of dating relationship for this long without having sex. This just wasn't typical for her. She thought back to their engagement party and the model Jaime, who had shown up and tried to spoil things. Dante's negative reaction to seeing her in attendance had been pretty strong. Lyra wondered if maybe he had some unresolved issues with Jaime holding him back where she was concerned. She wasn't interested in asking him about it because that would spoil the mood. Still, she hoped to inspire some fresh passion in her newly minted husband.

"Here we are," he said as they pulled up to the hotel's grand front entrance. He left the keys with the valet, and a bellhop took their bags for them. Lyra could tell that the front desk staff had immediately recognized Dante, even before he had given his name for the reservation. However minor, she had started to enjoy the extra attention of being with a celebrity. Dante knew that he was gorgeous. He also lavished praise on Lyra, pointing out how good they looked together. Touching a part of her body at all times, however lightly, just to maintain that physical connection.

When the elevator doors closed, Dante couldn't hold back any longer. He pressed her body against the elevator's back wall, kissing her fervently on the mouth. With his entire body contacting hers, she could feel that he was already hard.

"I just can't wait any longer," he told her, "and we're not going to answer any calls. I don't care who's trying to reach us."

"Good plan," agreed Lyra, kissing him back with unbridled enthusiasm.

As they stumbled into their suite, still kissing, they noticed that the staff had set up a bottle of champagne on ice. Two flutes waiting to be filled next to a plate of chocolate-covered strawberries. It was so romantic to see the champagne, but

Lyra wanted to make love to Dante first—there could be no more delays. By now, they were truly hungry for each other, and from this point onward, there would be no turning back.

Lyra undid the buttons down the front of his cotton shirt, after which he easily shrugged it off to reveal his beautiful pectoral muscles and rock-hard abs. She noticed that he had taken the care to wax his chest and back, which turned her on. His biceps were muscular, and he effortlessly picked her up and carried her to the bed. After placing her atop the duvet cover, he knelt on the floor at her feet. He carefully undid the small buckles on the ankle straps of her espadrilles, allowing her to gently kick off her shoes. He stood up, looking down at her. He quickly stepped out of his Italian leather loafers, then unbuttoned his trousers, watching her face the whole time and letting them fall to the floor. The look on his face was one of pure desire.

Now that he was down to his fitted boxer briefs, Lyra could see the full size of Dante's bulging erection, and she was impressed. At the bungalow, Dante had always worn trunks for swimming, so she had no idea how large his member was. She had been so turned on, thinking about what it would feel like to make love to him, for so long, that she knew it wouldn't take much for him to get her to that point of bliss. She reached up to pull him down on top of her, caressing his strong back, kissing his neck, teasingly pulling at his perfect nipples. She could feel his hands exploring their way up her thighs, under her dress, and finding her small, stretch lace, thong panties, which he expertly removed.

Since they were technically on their honeymoon, all Lyra had brought to wear were silk slip dresses and bikinis, not even any bras. This was a pleasant discovery for Dante as he gently slid her dress up her body and over her head to reveal her nubile form. This was the first time Dante had seen Lyra nude from head to toe, and he loved it. Her body was petite, her muscles were toned, and her arms were delicate. Her breasts were small and perky, just as he liked them, and her nipples were very responsive to his mouth as he sucked them at the same time as he caressed her breasts with his hands.

Dante was dying to penetrate her, and she probably would have been ready. Still, his ego held him in check: He wanted to show Lyra everything in his repertoire this afternoon and their lovemaking to be unforgettable. If he were to rush the experience, he felt it would be almost sinful. Lyra was the most intriguing and accomplished woman he had ever known. She had followed along in this crazy fake marriage scheme to satisfy his needs. Now, it was his turn to satisfy hers, and he intended to make it worth her while.

He left a trail of kisses up her chest and neck and returned to gently kissing her on the mouth and then more deeply. By now, his hands had traveled down her body, and he was touching her intimately. He could feel that she was already very wet, which excited him beyond measure. He enjoyed knowing that he had this power over her. For the past few weeks, he had sensed that Lyra had softened her stance toward him, and he felt that she was actually falling in love with him. The way Lyra was responding to his caresses confirmed for Dante that his inkling was correct.

As he slipped one finger inside her and then another, Lyra began to moan. He had removed his underwear by now, and she held his rock-hard penis in her hands. As she stroked it lightly, moving one hand up and down the shaft, Dante was afraid he might lose control and struggled to control his breathing. "Let's sixty-nine," he suggested as he rolled onto his back, inviting Lyra to turn around and place her delicate, hairless pussy over his face.

While Dante licked and sucked Lyra from below, she took his full, hard penis into her mouth. She gently and slowly moved her lips up and down, sometimes just sucking the tip and flicking it with her tongue, then switching to swirling her tongue all around the shaft, from top to bottom. She took short breaks to lick and suck his balls, which he enjoyed. Lyra was experiencing such a rush of pleasure from what Dante was doing to her that she almost found it difficult to maintain control while she was blowing him. Eventually, she felt her clitoris quiver with pleasure, and she allowed herself the time to enjoy her first orgasm at the hands of her new husband.

"Did you like that?" he asked her, knowing exactly what her answer would be.

"Please," was all she could say, and he reached for a condom that he had stealthily placed on the nightstand. He tore open the package with his beautiful white teeth, and Lyra helped him to roll it down over his perfect, glistening dick, still wet from her sucking. Then he lifted her pelvis from below and turned her legs sideways before plunging his erect penis into her. By now, Lyra was aching to feel him inside of her, and his lovemaking techniques were everything she had hoped for. This position allowed for deep penetration, almost blowing Lyra's mind. As he was thrusting, she watched how he held her legs, and she teasingly thought that he was such an excellent lover they should film it... that's how great he was.

After a few minutes like this, he turned her around to take her from behind. As he entered her from this angle, Lyra lowered her chest to the bed, which she knew would make her vagina feel tighter and more pleasurable for him. She could tell from his quickening breath and his change of pace that her technique had the desired effect. Lyra could feel another orgasm coming on. Just as she was about to let herself relax into it, she could felt that Dante was about to come too. Finally, they climaxed together, then collapsed onto the bed. Lyra enjoyed feeling his weight on top of her for just a few moments, and then he got up to dispose of the condom.

Before returning to bed, he poured each a glass of champagne and brought it to bed for them to enjoy a post-coital drink. As he handed her the glass, he leaned down to kiss her again, which solidified their newfound intimacy.

"We have great chemistry," Dante couldn't help but express his self-satisfaction. "How come it took us so long to figure this out?"

Lyra laughed, "I have no idea, and I kept hoping that you would just ravage me. I've been waiting for you to see the light."

"Oh, baby, I've seen the light," he growled as he started to kiss her again, which would inevitably lead to round two. "I suspect we're going to have an amazing mini-honeymoon."

Real Life

AFTER THEIR TIME in Dana Point, Dante and Lyra had no choice but to face reality and return to some semblance of normal life in Los Angeles. Araceli was still in the hospital, but she was getting closer to being well enough to fly home to France. Dante had been spending almost all of his time at Lyra's house. She had even created a workspace for him in her office so that he could efficiently conduct his business meetings remotely while she was at work. He still had Bungalow Five at the Beverly Hills Hotel, in case he and Lyra wanted a small, romantic escape and because Araceli's bags were still there. They had delayed the inevitable discussion of Dante's return to his home in France because neither of them wanted to broach that subject. Also, the point was moot because Araceli was still in the Los Angeles hospital.

By now, their relationship had started to feel organic and natural. They had fallen into a very nice, symbiotic pattern that was nothing like how they had started out. Neither of them had mentioned the NDA or the prenup, and they were too busy making love every night to discuss the dissolution of their make-believe marriage. Even with Lyra's teaching schedule and hospital routine, when they woke up early enough in the morning, if Dante had morning wood, she would climb on top and ride him for a good-morning quickie. It seemed they were making up for lost time and becoming more affectionate—seemingly more committed to one another —every day.

There had been one very sweet evening with Araceli. Dante had catered a gourmet, heart-friendly meal to the hospital so the three could all visit and look at the wedding photos. Araceli had made several references to future grand-children during that dinner, and Lyra and Dante had done their best to casually evade her questions. They hadn't had any discussion about their future together because each of them was secretly hoping that they could stay together. Still, they were both too shy to bring it up. It was easier to play coy with Araceli than to make up excuses. By now, neither of them planned to tell her the marriage was a sham, irrespective of her heart condition, because their feelings for one another had evolved into something real with long-term potential.

A few days later, having conferred with Araceli's entire medical team, Lyra determined that her body had sufficiently recovered and that she could be discharged from the hospital and safely fly home to Paris. She was ecstatic to hear this news and asked Lyra if she would accompany her home. She explained that having her cardiologist on board would give her comfort and peace of mind. Then she could show off her brilliant new daughter-in-law to all her Parisian friends.

"What do you think?" Lyra asked Dante.

"I think," he said, "that my incredibly hot wife should fly

my mother home and have a couple days of fun, shopping, and sightseeing in the City of Lights. Then hurry home before the end of the week to make me the happiest man on Earth."

She laughed, but what she wanted from Dante was an answer related to their marriage commitment. "I think there's another piece of the puzzle we need to resolve, don't you?"

"Lyra, if you haven't figured it out by now, I'll spell it out for you: I want you. In the beginning, this was clearly not my plan, but I love you, I need you, and I'm not going to let you go. Are you alright with that?"

Her shyness had prevented her from saying those words to Dante, and now she didn't have to. Her response was to kiss him deeply in agreement.

Lyra's short stay in Paris was a whirlwind. Araceli couldn't have been warmer or more effusive. Lyra was relieved to see that her energy had been completely restored. She and Dante did video chats throughout the day because they couldn't get enough of each other. Lyra felt giddy whenever she thought of him, and she loved knowing that he had fantasized about her all day. After their rocky start, they figured out that they were practically designed for each other. It was also nice to have a mother-in-law who was genuinely happy to welcome her into the fold.

When Lyra's flight landed in Los Angeles, she returned home to her empty house. Since Araceli had been discharged, she knew there was only one other place where Dante was likely to be. She made her way to the Beverly Hills Hotel, where she planned to surprise Dante, who thought she was on a later flight home. She had managed to get home on a better connection, and she knew Dante would be missing her intensely.

As she let herself in the door of Bungalow Five, she heard jazz music playing, but she saw no sign of Dante. Instead, she saw items of women's clothing strewn across the living room as if someone had purposely disrobed seductively. When she reached the French doors leading out to the private pool, she noted they were slightly ajar. Lyra thought for a moment that her eyes were fooling her. Still, she realized she was looking directly at Jaime, completely naked, lounging on an inflatable pool float. As their eyes met, Jaime's expression turned into a deliberate sneer. Without saying a word, Lyra turned on her heels. She walked blindly toward the bungalow's front door, where she bumped into Dante, who was entering, carrying a bottle of white wine and two glasses. She looked at him with tears in her eyes and just kept walking.

For his part, Dante was flummoxed. He had no idea what had just happened. All he knew was that Jaime had come over uninvited, asking for practical real estate advice about a condominium she wanted to purchase. He had gone to the bar to get some wine, just to be friendly, but he hadn't done anything inappropriate. He knew that Jaime had been a bitch to Lyra, but he had planned on talking to her for a half hour, then sending her away...for good.

Then he took a moment to look around and began to put the pieces together. He saw Jaime's shoes near the coffee table, her bra and panties on the loveseat, and her dress across the back of a chair. As he made his way out to the private pool deck, he had his smack-my-forehead moment when Jaime's long, lean, naked body came into view.

"Shit!" he exclaimed, dropping the bottle of wine and the stemware as he dashed out the door to follow Lyra. He wanted to catch her, to undo the damage before it was too late. Not bothering to speak to Jaime, he made a mental note to ask the hotel security personnel to come into the room and clear out Jaime and her belongings.

Making Up

IF EVER THERE was a time that Dante was happy to wear sporty shoes, it was now. He sprinted in his Gucci sneakers, his slim-cut linen trousers stressing a bit at the seams from the exertion of his muscular legs. "Lyra," he called out when he finally caught up to her in the lobby. By now, his white vee-neck tee shirt was soaked with sweat, and he was panting. She froze, and the look she gave him could have turned him to stone. He felt like her eyes were piercing right through his heart, which just happened to be breaking at the moment.

Lyra's mind was racing. All she could think about was how foolish she had been to allow herself to fall in love with a total playboy. How could she have let herself believe she was enough to tame Dante's wanton ways? It was public knowledge that he was a womanizer. Despite her multiple college degrees, she hadn't been intelligent enough to keep a clear head or to maintain her distance. She was so ashamed and brokenhearted and felt like an utter fool. God help her, despite everything, as she stood there motionless, watching him, waiting for him to speak, she still loved him. Her feelings weren't going away. She willed herself to hate him, but she couldn't.

Everyone in the lobby recognized Dante, and he knew by now that he was making a scene as a hush fell over the public space. However, at this point, he really didn't care, and he wasn't embarrassed because he wanted to make things right with Lyra. After everything they had been through, all the insanity of their non-relationship as it had evolved into an actual love story, the last thing he wanted was to lose her over a misunderstanding about Jaime, whom he could care less about.

"Lyra, please, listen to me," he continued. "She wasn't supposed to be in the pool. When I let her in, she was dressed, and I expected her to keep her clothes on. I don't know why she thought she could get naked, and then go in the pool. Lyra, it's you. You're all I want. I don't want Jaime. She asked me a question about a property she wanted to buy. I was going to sit with her for one glass of wine as a courtesy to an ex, then send her away. Please, Lyra, you've got to believe me. I love you so much. I've missed you. I wouldn't disrespect you that way, ever."

By now, everyone had taken out their phones and filmed their argument. Lyra dreaded the thought of having her dirty laundry aired on TMZ. This was not her idea of a happily ever after. She took a breath and tried to digest Dante's words. When she finally looked him in the eyes, she saw that he was crying, and her intuition told her he was being truthful. He stood a few feet away from her, with his hand outstretched, just waiting for her to come back towards him. It only took a few beats for her to relent, and she came over to place her hand in his.

"I believe you, and I love you, Dante," was all she needed to say and exactly what he needed to hear. They embraced, kissing and crying, and all the lobby guests started clapping.

This was the perfect ending to their make-believe romance and the ideal beginning for their real-life love story.

That's the end of the Can't Buy a Billionaire Series! Even though this series has finished, it doesn't mean the romance needs to. I'm thrilled to share another romance series with you! If you're looking for more love stories with royalty, office romance and friends to lovers, the *Saved by the Baby series* is your next binge read!

Love Was Never Part of Their Agreement

It was supposed to be a simple deal. An heir to protect Jaxson's fortune. His assistant Regina had always wanted kids. It seemed only natural to make a rather unusual arrangement.

But he never expected to fall in love...

Learn more about the Jaxson's and Regina's in Having Her Billionaire's Baby, Book One in the Saved by the Baby Series.

Start reading now!

Other Books by Rose M. Cooper

Can't Buy a Billionaire Series

About the Author

Rose M. Cooper read her first novel when she was eight years old. Since then, she has read tens of novels and twice as many short stories. She, however, did not discover her special knack for writing romance fiction until a decade later.

Now a full-time author with a specialty in contemporary romance, Cooper writes sensual yet relatable love stories designed to hook her readers at first glance. She views writing as another outlet to creativity, and thus has no intentions of setting down her pen just yet. There are many intriguing love stories to be told, and Cooper is set to tell them all.

She hails from New York and currently makes her home in Copiague, New York with her husband, her black cat and her Maine Coon cat. When she is not writing, you will most certainly find her around computers or getting her nose stuck in a book.

facebook.com/RoseMaeCooper

twitter.com/rosemaecooper

instagram.com/rosemaecooper

tiktok.com/@rosemaecooper

amazon.com/author/rosemaecooper

WANT TO BE FIRST TO KNOW?!

JOIN MY NEWSLETTER!
ROSEMAECOOPER.COM/NEWSLETTER

SUPPORT ME BY
LEAVING A REVIEW!

goodreads

amazon

BookBub